He gave a slow smile. "I don't *always* follow the rules."

"You don't?"

His gaze dropped again to her lips. "Not all of them."

The touch of his fingers sliding across her cheek and burrowing into her hair made her knees turn to water. "Are you about to break one right now?" she whispered.

"Oh, yeah." His head lowered until he was just a heartbeat away. "Can you guess which one?"

Rules. Who needed rules?

The second he touched his mouth to Stevie's he was lost. He'd fantasized about this kiss from the moment he saw her sitting on that suitcase looking so forlorn at the airport. Oh, he'd denied it, acting like some macho hulk who could take anything life dished out, but he couldn't pretend. Not anymore.

He was proving that. Right here. Right now.

Dear Reader

The inspiration for Matt and Stevie's story came as I read about a dengue fever outbreak in Rio de Janeiro, Brazil, about six hours from where I live. As I kind of shrugged and went about my daily business, I realised how different my life had become since moving to this beautiful country. I'm fortunate to live in a large city where healthcare is excellent, but I wondered how nonchalant I would be if I lived in a more remote region—such as portions of the Amazon River. DOCTOR'S GUIDE TO DATING IN THE JUNGLE is the result of those thoughts.

Thank you for joining Matt and Stevie as they experience the joy and heartbreak of working under very difficult conditions. Their dedication to their patients helps them rise to meet each new challenge. Best of all, this special couple finds love along the way. I hope you enjoy reading about their journey as much as I enjoyed writing about it!

Sincerely

Tina Beckett

DOCTOR'S GUIDE TO DATING IN THE JUNGLE

BY
TINA BECKETT

First published in Great Britain 2012
by Mills & Boon, an imprint of Harlequin (UK) Limited.
Harlequin (UK) Limited, Eton House, 18-24 Paradise Road,
Richmond, Surrey TW9 1SR

© Tina Beckett 2012

ISBN: 978 0 263 22656 0

Born to a family that was always on the move, **Tina Beckett** learned to pack a suitcase almost before she knew how to tie her shoes. Fortunately she met a man who also loved to travel, and she snapped him right up. Married for over twenty years, Tina has three wonderful children, and has lived in gorgeous places such as Portugal and Brazil.

Living where English reading material is difficult to find has its drawbacks, however. Tina had to come up with creative ways to satisfy her love for romance novels, so she picked up her pen and tried writing one. After her tenth book she realised she was hooked. She was officially a writer.

A three-time Golden Heart finalist, and fluent in Portuguese, Tina now divides her time between the United States and Brazil. She loves to use exotic locales as the backdrop for many of her stories. When she's not writing, you can find her either on horseback or soldering stained glass panels for her home.

Tina loves to hear from readers. You can contact her through her website, or 'friend' her on Facebook.

This is Tina's debut title
for Mills &Boon® Medical™ Romance

To my amazing husband, who believed I could succeed at anything I put my hand to.

With special thanks to my fabulous critique partners at Write Romance. I owe you ladies so much!

And to the amazing bunch of writers who hang out in Subcare over at eharlequin.com. The hand-holding and support found there is beyond compare.

CHAPTER ONE

'ALL we're doing is pasting a bandage over a gaping wound.'

Dr. Matt Palermo, in the middle of resectioning a femoral artery, ignored the exasperated mutter from the doctor beside him, knowing his colleague wasn't speaking literally. The neighboring gurney housed an injury just as frightening as the one Matt was working on. Except the patient's foot was long gone, lost somewhere in the depths of the rainforest.

The quick shrug of his shoulders had nothing to do with indifference and everything to do with dabbing a stray bead of perspiration that threatened to contaminate his surgical site. That was, if the sticky heat and buzzing flies hadn't already coated all the equipment with noxious bacteria.

He fought the frustration that rose in his throat. He knew exactly what the doctor to his left was going through. Hadn't he experienced the same overwhelming sense of hopelessness when he'd first come to this part of the Amazon? He still felt it at times. But that had had nothing to do with Brazil and everything to do with burying a large chunk of his heart in Tennessee. Even his bout with break-bone fever a couple of years ago couldn't compare to the agonizing phrase that had changed his life for ever: *I'm sorry; we did everything we could.*

He shook off the memory and eyed the newly closed artery, checking it manually for leaks. Satisfied with the job, he prepared to close.

'You need any help?' he asked, risking a quick glance at the other doctor, who now sat slumped in a chair while his patient slept on, unaware that life as he knew it was over.

Just like Matt's had been.

'I'm done.' Averted eyes and fingers scraping through hair that was stiff with a mixture of sweat and hair gel told Matt those two words would prove prophetic. After the city guy's two-week stint down the Amazon on the medical boat was over, he'd catch the first flight home to Chicago. He'd go back to his urban medical practice. Back to his pristine surgical suite and soft piped-in music. He wouldn't be coming back to Brazil.

Ever.

And Matt would again be left to fight the losing battle of man against nature.

Alone.

The blast of heat punched hard and fast as Stevie Wilson stepped from the cocooning shelter of the plane. She had to lock her knees and force herself to remain upright, or she'd end up melting onto the shiny black tarmac that danced and shimmered around her.

Wow. Coari was even hotter than she'd expected.

A quick tap of her hand sent her sunglasses toppling from their perch on her head to the bridge of her nose, where they cut the glare of the sun by half. She gave a sigh of relief and headed toward the worker who was busy tossing suitcases and foot lockers from the underbelly of the ancient aircraft.

'*Oi, Senhor! Cuidado com a mala vermelha, por favor.*'

The man smiled and gave her a thumbs-up signal, and then, despite her request to the contrary, dropped her medical bag with a *thunk* onto the growing mound of luggage.

She winced. 'Things can only get better from here, right, Stevie?'

Moving a few yards toward the vacant exterior of the airport terminal, she prayed someone was inside to meet her. She'd only dealt with the director of *Projeto Vida*, and though the woman had been cordial, she'd given a noncommittal 'Have the applicant e-mail his full résumé, including qualifications and a copy of his medical license. We'll get back to him.' She'd rung off before Stevie had a chance to admit the 'friend' she'd been calling for was actually herself.

Much to her shock, after sending in the requested information, she'd received an affirmative response, along with a list of necessary vaccinations and visa requirements. A month later, here she was.

Free and clear.

Free from her lying fiancé-cum-hospital-director and the political maelstrom that had arisen in the wake of their broken engagement. Free from the subtly averted eyes of the nursing staff that had torn at her heart and shredded her confidence.

She was free to do what she'd gone into medicine to do: treat those in need. And if traveling down the Amazon on a floating hospital ship was the only way she could meet that goal, so be it.

She tugged her sticky cotton shirt away from her body and fanned it against her ribcage, hoping her deodorant proved to be as Kevlar-strong as the ads claimed. A flatbed cart raced by, heading toward the growing mountain of luggage. Well, at least she didn't have to worry about unearthing the rest of her bags from that stack. Except that if her medical bag was now on top of the heap, it would soon be...

Turning, she took off at a sprint towards the pile and waved frantically at the two men. They stopped what they were doing, obviously wondering what the crazed foreigner was so upset about this time. She skidded to a stop and motioned to her bag, telling them what she wanted in Portuguese. Well, *continental* Portuguese, which she'd been told was different than the Brazilian version of the language, but it was all she had.

They evidently understood because the thumbs-up signs were again flashed in her direction before her bag was plucked from the stack and handed down—rather than tossed, this time.

'*Obrigada*.' She pulled a couple of small bills from her wallet and handed them to the men, directing them to her bags and asking if they'd bring them to the terminal for her. They nodded as she righted her case and set it on its wheels so she could tow it behind her.

A minute later, she was inside the main building, where the lack of air-conditioning—or even a fan—made the closed space seem more oppressive than the air outside. A rivulet of sweat ran down her back, lodging in the waistband of her low-rider jeans. Glancing around, she saw no one, other than employees and the fellow passengers who'd boarded the air taxi with her in Manaus. Stevie wondered for the first time if she'd made the right decision in coming. She'd expected—if not a giddy cheer by a pack of overworked doctors—at least one person to meet her at the airport and help her get to the boat.

Making her way to the desk, she asked if anyone had mentioned meeting a doctor here today.

'Ninguém, Senhora, desculpa.'

Not the answer she'd hoped to hear. She moved away from the counter and stood in the center of the room just as a wave of panic broke over the top of her. Despite her sensible flat sandals, her legs wobbled threateningly. Ignoring the scolding she'd just given the baggage handler over her medical bag, she shoved the telescoping handle into place and plunked herself down on the hard plastic casing. She dropped her handbag onto the cracked concrete floor beside her, wondering if she needed to put her head between her knees. No, then she might miss whoever was coming to pick her up. She settled for propping her elbows on her thighs and sinking her chin into her cupped palms.

Slow, deep breaths. That's it.

Surely she wasn't going to be abandoned.

A door on the other side of the building swung open and a man appeared, his gaze sweeping across the interior of the terminal as he strode toward the ticket counter. His height and close-fitting khaki slacks—as opposed to the uber-casual clothing worn by the male workers—marked him as an outsider. She couldn't quite see his eyes, but Stevie sat up straighter anyway and attempted a smile, praying this was her ride. But his glance merely clipped hers as he went by, a frown now marring the tanned flesh between thick, dark brows. He continued on to the desk and spoke in hushed tones, his black polo shirt pulling taut across powerful shoulders as he leaned over the counter. When the woman's hand swept in Stevie's direction, her heart leaped and she waved, stopping in midstream when he looked right past her.

As if she were invisible!

The flicker of hope went out, and she cringed at how desperate her madly waving arm must have appeared.

Desperate with a capital D.

She forced back her thoughts before they took a more destructive path. The man wasn't rejecting her personally, he was simply here to meet someone else.

'Onde?' he asked the woman at the counter, his voice loud enough for Stevie to hear this time.

'A loira sentada na mala, senhor.'

The blonde sitting on the suitcase? She glanced behind her just to be sure. There was no one sitting on a suitcase, except for...

The words slowly sank in. Oh, no. Surely not.

If her expression was horrified, the man's was doubly so. Triply so, if the brackets now etching the sides of his mouth were anything to go by.

He stalked toward her, every step appearing a battle of wills, one that he seemed determined to win. Stopping in front of her, he paused. 'Is this some kind of joke?'

'Excuse me?' Her neck had to crane back to look up at him, and her sunglasses slid off her head in the process, crashing to the floor. She ignored them, forcing herself to keep meeting those icy blue eyes.

'I'm here to meet Dr. Stefan Wilson,' he said, mangling her first name.

Stevie bit her lip, realizing just how tall he actually was, especially from her perch on the suitcase. If she weren't so worried about the still-shaky condition of her legs, she'd stand up. 'It's Stefani, not Stefan. 'Dr. *Stefani* Wilson. Most people call me Stevie, though.'

He shoved a hand through his hair and swore, before pulling a folded group of papers from one of his back trouser pockets. He took his time opening them and going over the documents. 'It says Stefan on the application. I was expecting a man.'

She gulped. Maybe he really was rejecting her.

Taking the papers he handed her, Stevie perused them, frowning over the missing 'i' on the application. So that's why he'd brushed her off earlier. 'I don't understand. I filled this out online and sent it to the director of *Projeto Vida* myself.'

She flipped the pages until she found her license. 'Here. See? It says Stefani, right here on my medical license. I also included a copy of my passport photo…hmm, which doesn't seem to be here either.'

'Great.' He took the papers and jammed them back into his pocket then looked off into the distance. 'Looks like the joke's on me.'

A woman.

Matt couldn't believe Tracy would have the nerve, when he'd specifically asked for a *male* doctor. She knew what this job was like. So far, no one—not even the last three men who'd signed up for the position—had been able to endure the tough working conditions. And Tracy thought this little scrap of a person could? That she'd be able to hack off a putrid, rotting leg, if the situation called for it?

He took in her white blouse, which clung to her curves wherever perspiration had gathered, becoming almost sheer in spots. At least it was thin and cool, which was so… *Practical* was the only word he allowed himself.

Even as the unlikely description bounced around his skull, he noticed a heavy droplet of moisture beside the coil of wheat-colored hair. As he watched, it slid down the side of her neck, gathering speed until it dipped into her collarbone. It hesitated as if unsure where to go next, then found the right path and headed down. Straight down. He swallowed and tore his eyes from the sight.

'Forget it. You're not staying.' He sent her a glare that he hoped would send her fleeing back to whatever cushy hospital job she'd left behind. If she was looking for adventure, she'd come to the wrong place. And he sure didn't need his mind wandering into areas it didn't belong.

'Forget it? You've got to be kidding me! I've just traveled four thousand miles to get here.' Her eyes flashed a warning. 'I'll have you know I'm a well-qualified vascular surgeon—'

'For which there's little use in the jungle.' He ignored the silent voice that reminded him he could have used her skills on the leg wound he'd treated a month and a half earlier.

'I've also done a year's residency in the emergency room, which means I'm well versed in the art of triage.'

'The *art* of triage?' He gave a hard laugh. 'It may be an art form where you come from, but battlefield triage is something completely different.'

Her head came up, and a vein in the damp skin just below her jaw pulsed with what could be either anger or fear. He'd bet fear. Good. That meant she'd soon be running back home, like Craig had done before her. And Mark before that.

And he'd bet his life he'd never *once* stared at a pulse point in either man's neck.

A baggage carrier came up behind them and set three giant red bags beside her, color-coordinated matches of the one she was currently sitting on. They were all spotless, evidently purchased just for this trip.

It figured.

He was surprised there weren't white roses embroidered across the fronts of them, or little save-the-rainforest slogans like the ones Craig had had on several of his T-shirts.

The carrier held up three fingers as if asking if these were all of her bags.

The woman in front of him gave the ubiquitous thumbs-up signal. The carrier nodded and hurried away without even waiting for a tip. Probably knew it was a lost cause.

Matt rolled his eyes. She knew nothing about this culture. 'I bet you don't even speak Portuguese.'

'Well, that's a bet you'd surely lose. And as far as 'battlefield triage' goes, the last time I checked my history books, Brazil was a pacifistic nation.' She scooped up the sunglasses, which lay broken on the floor, and dumped the remains into the open handbag that sat beside her. Picking up her purse, she stood to her feet, the top of her head barely reaching his chin.

'You can't learn everything about a country from a history book.'

'Ri-ght.'

The sing-song intonation she gave the word only served to tick him off further. *Women.* When he got hold of Tracy, he was going to give her hell.

But Tracy wasn't here at the moment, and Dr. Stefani Wilson was. 'I don't think you and this job are going to mesh.'

She hitched her handbag higher onto her shoulder, but there was now a hint of wariness in her gaze that made him frown. 'Is that right? You know…I don't believe I caught your name.'

'Matt. Matt Palermo.'

'Well, Mr. Palermo. Why don't you let me worry about whether the job and I are going to suit each other? If you'll just take me to Tracy Hinton—who evidently felt I was adequately qualified for this position—I'll soon be out of your hair.'

'Not bloody likely.'

'Meaning?'

'Two things. One, if you take this job you won't be "out of my hair" for a very long time. And, two, Tracy obviously didn't inform you of the living arrangements.'

'She spelled it out quite nicely. She and I will be living on a hospital boat, traveling from village to village. We'll be out for weeks at a time.'

'You…and Tracy.' He nodded, a small smile coming to his face when he realized she had no idea who he was. And he wondered if that was a simple mistake, or if Tracy had her hand in that as well.

'Yes. Why? Don't you think two women can handle the job?'

'What I think has no bearing on anything, or Tracy never would have hired you.'

'What an awful thing to say.'

'Not really. And Tracy won't be the one living with you.'

She blinked once, then again, his response evidently surprising her. 'Okay, so it'll be another doctor. It doesn't really matter who it is.'

'Doesn't it?'

A hand went to her stomach and she plucked at the hem of her shirt. 'Not at all.'

'So it wouldn't bother you to discover that we—you and I—will be living together, if you take this job.' He caught sight of a pale sliver of skin beneath her blouse as she fiddled with it. He forced the rest of the words from his suddenly dry mouth. 'We'll be under the same roof. For weeks at a time. Possibly months.'

She sucked down an audible breath and held it for a second or two before the muscles of her throat relaxed. 'I can handle it, if you can. Besides, there'll be another doctor on board to play chaperone, if you're worried about me throwing myself at you.' Her brows arched. 'Are you the ship's captain or something? The cook?'

He laughed. 'Unfortunately for you, it's neither of the above. And if you get on that boat, you'll have to put up with me 24-7.'

'Because?' Her teeth came down on her lower lip as if she realized something terrible was heading her way.

'Because *I'll* be your traveling companion, not Tracy. And I happen to be the only critical-care doctor within a hundred-mile radius.'

CHAPTER TWO

STEVIE perched on the seat of the Land Rover, keeping her body braced against the passenger side door as they navigated around the worst of the potholes. The ones they couldn't avoid, they plowed straight through.

With her teeth clicking together like castanets, she tried to gather her wits. Okay, so the introduction to her new job wasn't going quite like she'd expected. No cheering, no gratitude. Just a doctor who acted like he'd rather she drop off the face of the earth.

So what? She wasn't here to bask in anyone's praise. She'd come to help people.

The memory of Michael's laughter when she'd shown him the article on *Projeto Vida* swept through her mind. 'Seriously?' he'd said. 'What kind of person practices medicine in the jungle?'

Too embarrassed to admit she found the idea fascinating, she'd laughed along with him and had quickly blanked out the computer screen. The truth was, she'd toyed with the idea for the past year. She used to think Michael felt the same way, that he wanted to give back to those in need. Why else would he be at the helm of a public hospital?

Certainly not just to commandeer a private room for his little no-tell rendezvous, like the one she'd caught him having with a female doctor. On her birthday, of all things.

Humiliation and pain washed through her, bringing with it an inner scream of frustration. Why couldn't she get past this?

She must have made some sound because her new colleague's

head swiveled toward her. She squirmed in her seat before tilting her chin a bit higher.

Just because the good doctor wasn't thrilled about having her on board it didn't mean she should tuck her tail and go scurrying back to New York—no matter how much she wanted to right now. She'd agreed to stay for two years, and she intended to see them through, down to the very last day.

'So, why leave New York and come to our little neck of the rainforest?'

She gave a guilty start. He couldn't possibly know what she'd been thinking. 'Why do people normally do these types of things?'

His eyes searched hers before turning back to the road. 'Sometimes they don't think through the realities like they should.'

'And sometimes they just want to help.'

'Right. The last two doctors who "wanted to help," ended up leaving before they'd been here a month. It would have been better if they'd just mailed *Projeto Vida* a check.'

'Money can take the place of qualified doctors these days?'

His hands tightened on the wheel. 'No, but it doesn't help our cause when the faces change each time the boat pulls into a village.'

Interesting.

'You're talking about earning people's trust.'

'Yep. And it's mighty hard to come by these days.'

No kidding. She knew that for a fact.

She turned in her seat, her attitude softening a bit as she watched him shove a dark lock of hair off his forehead with an attitude of resignation. 'Every time someone leaves, you're the one who has to break the news to the villagers, aren't you? How long have you been with *Projeto Vida*?'

'Long enough.'

'Maybe it's time you started thinking about packing it in yourself, Dr. Palermo.'

'No.' He glanced back at her. 'And if you're going to take a trial run down the river with me, you'll need to call me Matt.

We try to be as informal as possible. The villagers will use your first name as well.'

She ignored the last part of his speech and concentrated on the first. 'Trial run? I signed up for two years.'

He grunted. 'So did the others.'

'Maybe I'm tougher than they were.' She smiled at him. 'Maybe I'm even as tough as you.'

Dark brows winged upward. 'Doubtful.'

'That sounds suspiciously like a challenge.'

'Does it?'

Stevie could swear his lips twitched as he said it and that the grooves where his frown lines sat became a little less pronounced. 'It does. And you might be sorry later, because I rarely back down from a challenge.'

Unless it came from her cheating ex as she'd hightailed it for the nearest exit. *If you leave now, you'll have a black mark on your record!* His shouted warning had cemented her decision to leave the hospital. To leave him.

'We'll soon see, won't we?' said Matt.

One of his tanned hands dropped from the wheel to the seat between them. There was a fresh cut across the knuckle of his middle finger that looked deep, and several old scars marring the back of his hand. Something about those hurts, old and new, made her stomach twist. This was a man who didn't play it safe. Who put his all into everything he did. That was something Stevie could relate to. She'd gained a few new scars of her own over the last month or so.

'You use protection, don't you?'

He glanced over, eyebrows high. 'Excuse me?'

Oops. That hadn't come out right.

'Surgical gloves,' she clarified, touching a spot just beneath his cut, not sure where the urge came from. 'Especially when you have injuries.'

He curled his fingers into a fist, the muscles in his forearm bunching. 'Of course.'

'Good.' She gave a brisk nod as if the heat from his skin hadn't just singed her. As if she wasn't scrubbing her fingertips across her thigh in a vain attempt to remove the sensation.

He frowned, and Stevie realized he'd seen her reaction. Heat prickled along her scalp, and she turned her head to look out at the scenery. 'How long until we get to the boat?'

'About a half-hour.' They hit another pothole, and she scrabbled for a handhold to avoid careening off the seat and onto the floorboards.

'Sorry,' he said. 'I keep forgetting you're not used to roads like this.'

'It's okay. At least it's not one big construction zone, like in New York.'

'Which is why the roads there don't swallow small children.'

She blinked. Wow, did the man actually have a sense of humor? Her mouth opened to respond when his cellphone went off.

He braked, fumbling to pull the phone from the holder on his belt. Stevie glanced back to make sure there were no cars heading their way, but the road was deserted, which made it odd that he'd stopped at all. Maybe he was a little more cautious than she'd thought.

''Ello?' He listened for a few seconds looking straight ahead. 'Yep, she's here. Listen, I told you what I wanted. Surely there were other appli—'

He sighed. 'Just keep looking, will you?'

Her brows went up. So much for his 'changing faces isn't good for the cause' spiel. It didn't stop him from trying to swap her face for someone else's post haste. Which meant she'd be out of a job, unless she went crawling back to Michael.

Fat chance of that happening.

'I don't know. She had quite a pile of suitcases, but she didn't say anything about... Hold on.' Matt pulled the phone away from his ear, glancing her way. 'Mosquito nets?'

She nodded. 'A hundred and fifty of them, just like Tracy asked for. I also brought a case of repellent wipes for use on board the boat.' She frowned. 'Don't tell me you actually thought I had clothes in all those suitcases?'

* * *

Matt suddenly found himself unable to meet her eyes. Okay, so he'd misjudged her on one count. 'Yeah, she brought them,' he said into the phone.

'Good,' said Tracy. A few seconds of silence crawled by. 'Listen, give her a chance, will you? You and I both know you need another doctor on that boat. So don't say anything stupid.' A laugh rose in his throat, which he quickly suppressed. Too late. He'd already said several stupid things. And for the past few minutes he'd suddenly realized how lonely his job was. The simple touch of Stefani's fingers and the concern in her voice when she'd noticed the scratch on his hand had hit him in a dark corner of his mind.

He sent her a quick glance to find her staring out the side window in an obvious attempt not to eavesdrop. A long strand of hair had come loose from her bun and now trailed down her cheek, the tip curling just above her shoulder.

A strange sense of longing swept over him. What had Tracy been thinking, sending a woman? Didn't she realize how flammable this situation could become? He tried to snuff out the image of Stefani's long nimble fingers sliding across his skin, her surgeon's brain dissecting and memorizing his every reaction. Or her long dark lashes fluttering shut as he...

He shook his head, realizing Tracy was waiting for his response. 'Right. "Don't say anything stupid." I'll do my best.'

She laughed. 'Don't make me come down there.'

As much as he wanted Tracy to witness her folly firsthand, he knew he couldn't afford to hang around the port and do nothing. Waiting for Stefani's arrival had already put him two days behind schedule, and he had people counting on him. As soon as they got to the boat, they needed to be on their way.

'Your concern is duly noted, but I'm a big boy, in case you haven't noticed.'

'Oh, I have. And I'm counting on you to act like one.'

Paint—long peeling ribbons of white—clung to portions of the boat. Other sections were laid bare, like bones stripped of their flesh. Stevie could have been looking in a mirror at her own reflection.

She was pretty sure this wasn't what Matt had in mind when he'd mentioned battlefield triage, but the vessel certainly looked like it had been through a warzone.

And come out on the losing end.

This couldn't be the medical boat. She tugged the doorhandle on the Land Rover and stepped out of the car, while Matt went around and hauled her luggage from the back of the vehicle.

The wall-to-wall grins on the faces of two men who'd disembarked from the ship and now hurried toward them said her premonition was correct. This vessel was indeed going to be her home for the next two weeks. Who was she kidding? Try two years. She shut her eyes and sent up a quick prayer. She'd put her name on a contract, effectively signing away her life. She'd see the far side of thirty before she left Brazil.

Matt smiled at the new arrivals and clapped each of them on the back before introducing them to her. 'Nilson and Tiago, this is Stefani Wilson, the newest member of our team.'

Everything was said in Portuguese, so she should have understood it easily, but Stevie found herself having to concentrate to make out the words through their thick accents. But they were friendly and welcoming, more than she could say for Matt. The two crew members gathered up her luggage as if it weighed no more than a couple of sacks of groceries and took off toward the ship.

She bit her lip, her hopes of being mistaken fading. Even if the men weren't already scampering up the gangplank, the raggedy lettering on the back of the boat spelled her fate out in no uncertain terms: *Projeto Vida*. This was the medical ship, for better or worse.

'Home, sweet home.' Low graveled tones slid across her senses like calloused hands moving over soft skin.

Palpable. Dangerous.

Shivering, she glanced up to find his attention fastened on the boat and not on her. Anything that could wring that kind of reaction out of the man couldn't be all bad. Right?

Maybe she should try to see the ship from his perspective. 'So this is it, then?'

He nodded, the warm affection in his eyes cooling as he studied her face. 'Ready to run away yet?'

'I don't run.'

'No?'

The way he said it made her wonder if he knew more about her situation than he was letting on. But so what if he did? She had nothing to hide.

Except for the tattered remnants of her heart. And the disciplinary note in her file.

Her lips tightened. She wasn't hiding those either. She'd told Tracy that her 'friend' had had a run-in with his hospital, but that he'd done nothing wrong. Why, then, had she hidden her identity at first? Though, after receiving her résumé, Tracy had to have realized Stevie had been talking about herself on the phone that day.

'No, I'm not going to run.' Not this time. Not even if the boat had the name 'Typhoid Mary' inscribed on its side.

She slapped at a mosquito on her arm and immediately wondered if it was a carrier of some deadly ailment. Running didn't seem like such a bad option all of a sudden.

'You'll need to wear repellent. They seem to attack newcomers more than residents. Must have sweeter blood or something.'

'I bet they don't attack you at all,' she said, then realized how childish the words sounded.

A muscle worked in his jaw and one hand went to the back of his neck and rubbed as if trying to ease a knot from the firm muscles. 'Ready to get to work?'

'That's why I'm here.' The sharp tone made her cringe. 'Ugh, sorry. Chalk up my bad manners to jet lag, okay?'

'No problem.' He lowered his hand and rotated his neck half a turn. Stevie heard several soft pops as the vertebrae along it cracked. He gave a low groan of relief.

'Do you have back problems?' No way would she admit she'd begun her education in chiropractic before switching to traditional medicine.

'Nothing serious. Just getting old.' But even as he said it, she noticed he slightly twisted his upper body—instead of just his neck—when looking down at her, a classic sign of pain. He'd been fine in the car when glancing over at her, so it was limited to one side. Her brain worked through possible diagnoses before she stopped herself.

It's none of your business, Stevie. Just leave it be.

'Shall we go aboard?' she asked.

'If you're sure you're up for it.'

Something about the way he said it made prickles rise along the nape of her neck. Surely the inside of the boat couldn't be in worse condition than the outside. She could understand being busy, but lack of hygiene and sterility were things she wouldn't stand for.

Once she stepped from the rickety dock onto the boat, her heart sank. More peeling paint and the deck's wooden surface was gouged and pitted. 'You see patients onboard?'

'Yes, in the exam-room-slash-surgical-suite.'

Surgical suite. Wow. And maybe they still bored holes in skulls, too. She forced her tongue to the roof of her mouth and held it there, where it couldn't flap around and say things she would later regret.

Their next stop was the galley. Stevie was relieved to find the food preparation area neat and tidy. 'Where do you get your drinking water?'

'The river. The filtration unit on the counter was donated by a relief agency. It's a three-stage system that filters out particles and then zaps the water with UV rays to kill most bacteria. We can send it through an additional stage that injects a chlorine solution in areas where cholera is endemic.' A lean finger hooked around the handle of an empty plastic bottle and lifted it. 'Before the filter, we had to carry clean water aboard in these, which made scrubbing for surgery a complicated affair.'

'I can imagine.' She wandered over to the rectangular unit. The metal casing was spotlessly clean. She relaxed a bit. Maybe things wouldn't be as bad as she'd feared. 'I knew filters like this existed, but wow. It looks like something NASA would have.'

'I hear the system used on the space station is similar.'

Matt lounged against a nearby doorframe, one shoulder propped against the wooden surface, observing her. Although lean, his body filled the opening, his dark silky hair brushing the top of the frame. She swallowed, feeling trapped all of a sudden and not sure why. He wasn't threatening in a scary kind of way.

She rephrased that thought. He was scary, but only because he made her blood rush through her veins simply by looking at her. And that made the man doubly dangerous, since she could no longer trust herself to make wise choices when it came to the opposite sex. Meeting problems head on might work for some people, but for Stevie, avoidance was now the name of the game. And that included avoiding the six-foot-two-inch problem who stood right in front of her.

'Com licença, Mateus.' The voice came from behind him, and Matt moved into the room to let the crew members pass.

Mateus, the Portuguese equivalent of Matthew.

So they *did* go by first names, just like Matt had said. She liked that. Michael would have insisted on formality at all costs. He'd said that to get respect, you had to demand respect. She used to agree, but now she wondered. That kind of respect could be lost in the blink of an eye—or behind the closed doors of an examination room. Besides, she sensed an admiration from these men that wasn't a result of social standing or titles, but something earned through time and trust.

Would she ever be included in their little circle? Probably not.

'We've put the new doctor's bags in your room.'

Dull color crept into Matt's face, and Stevie sensed her scalp heating as well. They'd put her bags in *his* room? She hovered between saying 'Thank you' and squeaking out the protest that scrabbled up her throat, seeking the nearest exit. Before she could do either, Matt wrapped a hand around her upper arm. 'I'll show you where your things are.'

As soon as they were through the door, she planted her heels to stop their forward motion, ignoring the way the warmth from his fingers burrowed beneath her skin. Uh-oh. There went that blood-rushing-through-the-veins sensation again.

She tugged free of his hold, furious with herself for having any kind of reaction at all.

'Why did they put my suitcases in your room? I don't know what's going on, but—'

'Not here. Let's get out of earshot, okay? They've already got enough to gossip about for the next two weeks. We all thought the new doctor was going to be...well, a man. Now you see why it's so complicated.'

She didn't. Not at all. 'Just have them move my bags to another room.'

His brows went up. 'You'd rather sleep with Nilson and Tiago in the crew's quarters, then?'

'What? No, of course not. There must be somewhere else.'

He walked down the narrow aisle, forcing her to follow him. She noted he had to hunch his shoulders to accommodate the low ceiling. 'There's not. The space is cramped as it is, there are no extra rooms.'

No wonder he'd flipped out when he'd realized 'Stefan' was a woman. Kind of hard to avoid someone when you had to share a bedroom with him. What was she going to do? Lordy, what if he only had one bed in that room?

She'd camp on deck if she had to.

And risk being devoured by mosquitoes?

Maybe.

They came to a doorway, and her heart raced as Matt pushed it open, motioning her through. She squeezed by him, careful not to touch, but all the precautions in the world couldn't prepare her for the clean masculine scent that followed her into the room. It permeated the space, branding everything in it as his. If she stayed here, would it mark her as well?

She swallowed and forced herself to take shallow breaths as she examined the room. Even with her suitcases piled one on top of the other in the corner, there was barely enough room for two people to stand, much less move about.

She went slack with relief, however, when she spotted two beds, rather than one. Thick woven hammocks, actually, one above the other. A shared mosquito net hung suspended from a hook, tied to the side with a worn bungee cord at the moment. But at night it would be set free, encasing both hammocks in a tight intimate circle. As if they were in their own little world.

Her hard-won composure finally cracked, allowing panic to ooze between the gaps as she stared at the folded blanket and pillow resting on the bottom hammock. A worn paperback—Tom Clancy's *The Sum of All Fears*—lay on top of the bedding. How apropos that title was.

Matt had mentioned seeing how tough she really was. They were about to find out.

Her laugh, when it came, was one cackle short of hysterical. 'Well, I guess this means you want me on top.'

CHAPTER THREE

HER on top? Matt pinched the bridge of his nose, trying to eradicate the image that sprang to mind.

'Don't worry, I'll bunk with the crew,' he said, his voice coming out as a croak.

She swung around, her green eyes shining with relief. 'But if their room is as small as this one...'

'We'll make do. I'll hang a third set of hooks above theirs for my hammock.'

She eyed the beds. 'That will put you almost flush against the ceiling. You'll have no room to move.'

Yeah, almost like being inside a fabric coffin. His fingers massaged his neck muscles, trying to get rid of the ache that just wouldn't quit. 'Whatever it takes.'

'You are aware that hot air rises, right? I'm already dripping with sweat, and I'm on the floor.' Her eyes went to the ceiling. 'It'll be like being in a slow roaster up there.'

Exasperation washed over him, and he dropped his hand, allowing it to slap against his thigh. 'Thanks for pointing out all the positive aspects of our situation.'

'No problem.' She licked her lips and paused. 'Listen, we're both adults, and it's not like you'll be able to see...anything once I'm in bed. I can wear gym shorts and a T-shirt rather than my PJs. If we leave the door open at night and restrict our dressing and undressing to the bathroom, we should be fine.'

Good suggestion—except that Matt didn't normally wear *anything* to bed. And he wasn't sure how he felt about looking up at night, knowing those sweet curves were lying just over his head, close enough so that all he had to do was reach up and...

'Give me a couple hours to think it over.' He backed out of the room and into the hallway.

She shrugged as if he were the one with the problem, not her. 'Suit yourself. Don't say I didn't offer.'

It would almost be better if she'd wiggled her hips and implied that the offer went beyond mere sleeping arrangements. Then he could ship her butt back to Manaus with a clean conscience. The last thing anyone needed was a messy two-week fling. And a long-term relationship was out of the question. Vickie had been it for him. Now that she was gone...

He had no doubt Stefani would be going home at the end of those two weeks, if not before. Even if she didn't turn tail and run, he'd already asked Tracy to keep looking for a replacement. Surely Stefani could understand his concerns now that she'd seen the conditions. It wasn't just him, he had the crew to think about—and some of the tribes were bound to have a problem with him bringing in an unattached female. If the vessel were bigger, having team members of the opposite sex might be more feasible. Or if he and Stephani were married...

Who was he kidding? Even the thought of marriage made his stomach tighten with dread.

'How about showing me the rest of the facilities?' she said, forcing his mind back to the situation at hand.

'Sure. Let me tell the men to get under way first.' He paused. 'Unless you'd like to go back to the airport now that you've seen the boat?'

Her shoulders straightened. 'I knew what I was signing on for.'

'That would normally be my cue to argue and give you one more chance to change your mind, but we're already behind schedule. And, as Tracy continually reminds me, I really could use the help. I'll be right back.'

Once he asked Nilson to cast off, he gave Stefani the tour, stopping by the restrooms first. He suppressed a smile when her nose wrinkled at the mention of river water being pumped in for showers. 'We do run it through a filter, so you won't find anything crawling through your hair when you're done.'

'Ugh. It's better *not* to put images like that in my head.'

When they arrived at the examination room, her eyes widened. 'This is amazing.' She glanced up at him. 'I have to admit, you had me worried for a while.'

He peered at the room, trying to see the space through her eyes. 'How so?'

'When I saw the outside of the boat and the…er, restroom… Let's just say I wondered what I might find in here. But it's spotless.' She touched the gleaming chrome handle of the scrub sink. 'Does this water come from the river as well?'

'Yes, but it goes through a steam process, then stored in a sterile tank prior to use.'

'It seems you've thought of everything. How are the instruments sterilized?'

'Same method. Afterwards, they're shrink-wrapped into kits. It's time-consuming, but we don't do many surgeries.'

She tucked a stray wisp of hair behind her ear, drawing his attention to her high cheekbones and long dark lashes. There was a china-doll delicacy to her that made him wonder what crazy impulse had led her to sign up for a tour down the Amazon. Was she trying to prove something to herself? To someone else?

Wandering to the center of the room, she paused between the twin stainless-steel exam tables. 'These are top of the line. This set up must have cost a small fortune.'

'Yes. Which is why the rest of the boat looks a little worse for wear.' It was a half-truth, and he wasn't sure why he felt the need to defend the ship's condition, but now that the words were out, he stubbornly expanded on them. 'We put as much money as possible into caring for our patients. As long as the ship is solid and in good mechanical order, I figure the doctors and crew can afford to scrimp on the little things.'

She laughed. 'Like real beds.'

'Actually, no. Hammocks are more practical. No risk of bedbug infestations or other creepy crawlies that can hide inside a mattress. And they're cooler than traditional beds. I think you'll be surprised at how comfortable they are.'

He omitted the fact that the beds swung gently with every movement, whether that movement came from the boat or from other, more sensual, activities.

She tilted her head and looked up at him as if she could read his thoughts. 'I'll have to re-evaluate some of my opinions.'

Time to put some space between them and the subject of beds. 'Anyway, as far as this particular room goes, we need to keep the risk of contamination to a minimum. Which means access is limited to doctors and patients.'

'Understood. Do you ever keep patients overnight?'

'On occasion. If we've had to operate, for example. Or if...' he forced air into his lungs '...one of the team becomes ill and we have to transport them to a major city.'

She paused, her eyes sliding across his face. Her pupils dilated, and compassion flared within their depths. 'You've had to do that, haven't you? Transport a team member.'

He couldn't go down this road. Not today. Trying to head off any further questions, he checked his watch, relieved to find it was almost noon. 'Let's go see what Tiago has come up with for lunch.'

Lunch turned out to be a one-pot meal called *carurú do Pará,* featuring dried shrimp and okra. It was unlike anything she'd ever tasted, but delicious just the same.

'Do you like it?' Matt asked, forking a piece of shrimp into his mouth.

'It's wonderful. I've never had okra in anything but jambalaya.'

Tiago, who she'd found out was the team's cook, nodded. 'Good, yes?'

Reverting to Portuguese, she asked what other kinds of dishes were popular in the region. Smiling, he rattled off several names, but the words were unfamiliar. It was amazing how two languages could be the same and yet so very different.

Matt must have noticed her confusion as well. Keeping the

conversation going in Portuguese, he asked, 'Your accent is different. Where did you learn the language?'

'I lived in Portugal for seven years as a child. My father worked at the American Embassy.'

'That explains it.'

His furrowed brow made her sit a bit taller. 'Is there something wrong with the way I speak?'

'Not at all. But you'll find sentence construction is a little different here.'

'I've noticed.'

Tiago spoke up. 'I think your accent is very nice, Miss Stefani.'

She smiled her thanks. 'Stefani is my formal name, but all my friends call me Stevie. Won't you do the same?'

'Sh-tée-vee?' He struggled to get the name out, and she noticed Nilson—busy manning the helm, his plate balanced on the control panel—mouthed the word as well.

'Perfect,' she said.

Matt just shook his head. 'From Stefan, to Stefani, to Stevie. No wonder I was confused about your gender.'

'And now? Are you still confused?'

'Confused?' His lips tilted in a sardonic smile. 'More than ever.'

With that cryptic statement he stood and walked to the sink, carrying his plate. Since Tiago and Nilson followed his lead, she shoveled one last mouthful of the delicious meal into her mouth and stood as well. 'Thank you so much for lunch. It was wonderful.'

'I'm glad you liked it.' After Matt ducked through the door, Tiago leaned in a bit closer and whispered, 'I think you will be good for Mateus. He misses his wife very much.'

Wife? Matt was married? Oh, Lordy, and she'd practically insisted on playing share-sies with his bedroom. What was she thinking?

'Where is she? His wife, I mean.' The words were out before she could stop them. But she wanted to know. Because other arrangements definitely had to be made. No wonder he'd offered to sleep with the crew. Her face flamed. She'd told him not to worry about her throwing herself at him and yet she'd offered to sleep right above the man's head. Surely he didn't think—

'His wife is…she's…' Tiago bowed his head and pointed skyward.

'What? I don't understand.' Her eyes widened as she realized what he was trying to say. 'Oh. I'm so sorry.'

He waved his hands in front of him. 'Please don't speak of it with him. He might not like that I told you.'

'Of course not.' She glanced at the empty doorway, hoping Matt wasn't lurking outside. She wanted to ask some additional questions, like when and how his wife had died, but she didn't want to get Tiago in trouble. She also didn't feel right indulging in gossip behind Matt's back. If he wanted her to know, he'd tell her.

Although why would he? He'd made it pretty obvious he didn't want her here, and he certainly didn't expect her to last very long.

She hurried to catch up with him and found him on deck staring out at the dark waters of the *Rio Preto.* 'When do we reach our first stop?'

'Some time tomorrow afternoon.' He turned toward her, propping a hip against the rail and crossing his arms over his chest. 'Do you mind if I ask you something?'

Thinking of the personal information she'd just learned about his wife, she hesitated, wondering if he was going to ask about her last job—or whether she was involved with someone. 'I suppose not.'

'Why did you choose Brazil?'

Relief washed over her. That was easy. 'I knew the language.' She crinkled her nose. 'Well, kind of.'

His lips curved, and she caught a quick flash of teeth. 'There is that. But that's not exactly what I mean. As a vascular surgeon you could have gone to any hospital in the world. But this…' his hand swept to the side, indicating the river '…is a little outside your specialty, don't you think?'

She shrugged, forcing herself to smile back. 'Maybe I wanted to expand my horizons.'

'Surely there were other ways you could have done that.'

Her options had been rather limited when she'd called Tracy and inquired about the position, but she was loath to tell him that. At least at the moment. 'Possibly. Why does it matter?'

His eyes slid over her face, pausing at her lips before coming back up to meet her gaze. 'Just curious.'

'What about you? Why did you come here?' If he could pose the question, then it seemed only fair she should get a chance to do the same. Besides, it would move him away from this particular subject. And a part of her hoped he'd tell her about his wife, and get it out in the open.

'It was something I've wanted to do ever since med school.'

She nodded. 'Did you specialize?'

'Nope. Although, looking back, maybe I should have.'

'I imagine you've learned more here than some doctors learn in a lifetime.'

A muscle worked in his jaw. 'Maybe more than I wanted to.'

Something about those words made her heart clench. Was he talking about his wife's death? Now was probably not the time to ask.

'So we reach our first stop tomorrow.'

'Yep. We'll need to figure out how to introduce you to the villagers, if there are any questions about your presence.'

'What do you mean?'

He shrugged. 'Let's just say some of the tribes are more conservative than others.'

'They don't think women should be doctors?'

'Some of the chiefs might have trouble with us traveling together.' He studied her. 'You don't happen to have a husband stowed in your luggage, do you?'

A shaft of pain went through her, and it took her a second or two to respond. 'Nope, sorry. You've never brought a woman with you?'

'Not a female doctor, no.' He uncrossed his arms and straightened. 'But we can talk more about it later. You must be tired.'

'A little, but I'm okay. Is there something you want me to do?'

'Not at the moment. Tiago and Nilson are pretty proprietary

about the day-to-day boat chores. If you try to pitch in, they'll be offended. Let me think…'

He smiled suddenly, his eyes crinkling as he motioned toward one of her bare arms. 'You could always lie on deck and work on your tan. Try to blend in a little more.'

She laughed, the tension between them defusing. 'Nice try, Tarzan. With three guys roaming the place? Hardly. Besides, as you can tell by my vampire-like skin tones, the sun and I are sworn enemies. Even if I *could* tan, baking in this heat doesn't really appeal to me.'

'There's a wall-mounted fan in our…in the bedroom. You can read, then, or relax. Unpack.'

'What are you going to do?'

'Go over the navigational charts with Nilson.' He tugged at a chain around his neck and retrieved two keys from beneath his shirt. Unhooking one of them, he held it out. 'This is to the exam room. You'll need to put it somewhere safe. The door and medicine cabinets are keyed alike, so it works on both. The crew members can be trusted but, because of the drugs we keep on hand, it's better not to put temptation in anyone's way. So you and I will have the only copies.'

Her fingers brushed over his palm as she took the key from him, shivering as she noted the metal was still warm from resting against his skin. When he allowed his own key to slide back beneath his polo shirt, the image of steel pressed against a hard wall of flesh caused her to take a quick step back.

'Do you have a chain to hang it from?' Matt's gaze slid to her chest, and then jerked back to her face.

Had he just pictured the key nestled between her breasts? That would actually be a relief considering her response a few seconds ago. How humiliating would it be for her to nearly swoon over the stupid heat of a key and not have him notice her at all?

She glanced at his face, looking for confirmation.

Nothing. There wasn't a hint of interest behind those cool blue eyes.

The pendulum swung back toward humiliation. What kind of woman broke off her engagement and immediately started checking out every guy in town? Well, technically she was only checking out one guy in this particular area, but still.

She curled her fingers into her palms, allowing her nails to dig into her skin. 'I have something in one of my bags. I'll use that.'

'I'll leave you to it, then,' he said.

At her nod, he turned and walked away, and she couldn't help but notice the loose-limbed gait, which spoke of easy confidence, or the way his muscles flexed as he gripped the top of the doorjamb and ducked beneath as he headed down the hall.

As soon as the dark recesses of the boat swallowed him completely, she sagged against the railing and held the key to her chest.

What on earth was wrong with her?

Once they reached the first village, she'd be far too busy to think of anything but her patients. At least she hoped so.

Her mouth twisted. She'd forgotten to ask where Matt and the crew lived between trips down the Amazon. Surely they didn't stay on the ship year round.

And if they did? Could she live aboard this boat…in the same room with Matt…for the next two years?

Oh, boy. She didn't think so.

Because if she thought he was attractive now, when her instincts were on high alert, what would happen if she let her guard down even a little?

I don't run.

The words she'd thrown at him swirled around her, calling her a liar. Because if she couldn't get her silly libido under control, that's exactly what she was going to do.

Run.

CHAPTER FOUR

MATT awoke to something nudging his side. He opened one eye and squinted sideways, encountering a worn pair of flip-flops.

Tanned skin, calloused feet.

Not the creamy white toes sporting pale pink polish that had driven him from his hammock in the middle of the night. He'd decided it was safer to remain on deck.

'Why are you sleeping here, Mateus?'

Ah, yes, the question of the century, and one he'd prefer not to answer at the moment.

He shoved back the mosquito netting that was now tangled around him like a shroud and found Tiago, who stood with one hand scrubbing the top of his head, obviously still half-asleep.

'It's cooler,' Matt muttered.

The young man snorted. 'Really? On the Amazon, it is not cool anywhere.'

He had a point, but Matt chose to ignore it. 'It's still dark. Why are you up so early?'

'I heard a noise on deck and wanted to make sure everything was secure.'

Hmm…that would have been a better answer than his own response. 'Everything's fine.'

'Why do you not just stay in my quarters?'

Because Matt hadn't been able to resist answering Stevie's subtle challenge. *She* was adult enough to stay in a room with someone of the opposite sex, therefore he was determined to do the same. Only it hadn't worked out quite like he'd hoped.

He sat up and rubbed his hand over his face, trying to erase the image of that smooth white calf and ankle that had appeared over the side of Stevie's hammock and dangled close enough to give him nightmares of a different sort. And that damned sparkly polish on her toes hadn't helped. He'd nearly fallen out of bed in his rush to put some distance between them.

He sighed, trying to disguise the sound. 'Your quarters are cramped enough as it is.'

'What about the infirmary?'

'I'm fine.'

Tiago frowned. 'I know you want to keep the germs out, but you can't sleep on the hard deck for two weeks. What about your back? I can see it still bothers you.'

That was something Matt didn't want to talk about either. 'I'll survive.'

'But if you hurt it again, you might have to—'

'Go back to bed. We'll figure something else out in the morning.'

The other man tsked, but nodded. 'I'll at least hang the netting, so it does not strangle you in the night. Besides, the mosquitoes can feed right through it.'

The thing was so tangled, it probably provided a pretty good barrier, but he got up and helped Tiago suspend the midpoint from some fishing line and tack it to the wooden railing next to his makeshift pallet. Tiago was right, the netting was better this way.

Saying goodnight, Matt watched as the other man trudged back down the dark passageway to his own comfortable hammock, passing the quarters where Stevie was currently sleeping. Was her leg still on decadent display?

Forget it. He scooted beneath the netting and flopped down onto his blanket. That was another thing. He was used to sleeping in the buff and without the benefit of blankets. The additional coverings made him feel claustrophobic and hot. What had Tracy been thinking?

She hadn't been. That much was obvious.

But would it have bothered him as much if Tracy herself had come and stayed on the boat? If they'd shared a room?

No, because not only was she Vickie's sister, she was also a good friend. There was no attraction getting in the way of their work. Unlike with Stevie.

He snorted. Who said Stevie was attracted to him? Maybe it was purely a one-way street.

That wasn't the only thing bothering him. He still had to figure out what they were going to tell the tribes when they went ashore tomorrow.

Maybe no one would even ask about Stevie. And if they did? What then?

He'd only been half joking when he asked Stevie if she was hiding a husband inside one of her suitcases. Because it would make it so much easier if there was one.

Or if Matt could simply say he'd gotten married again.

He blinked. Maybe he had. Or he could pretend he had.

No one had to know that he wasn't bringing his new bride—who also happened to be a doctor—with him. Vickie had been a nurse, and they'd traveled together. No one thought a thing of it.

Would Stevie even agree to the ruse? He could tell her it was either that or she could go home. It was the truth, because he sure as hell couldn't think of another story that would take care of any questions with one fell swoop.

And what about him? Would he be able to pretend to be Stevie's husband, knowing he'd have to learn more about her to make their tale believable?

Putting his hands behind his head, he tried to go back to sleep and ignore what that would entail.

Matt Palermo, permanently grieving widower, might have to break his one iron-clad rule about women.

Don't get too close—ever.

Her dad spun her around and around, holding her suspended by one arm and leg, while her other limbs dangled in space. She half giggled, half screamed and then thrashed around when she realized the swaying hadn't been solely in her dreams. And her wiggling had just caused her to overbalance...

Scrambling, she clawed at the hammock with her hands, succeeding in grabbing the open woven fabric just as the whole contraption inverted itself. She found herself hanging upside down, her legs automatically wrapping around the center of the hammock and locking together at the ankles. She tightened her fingers to avoid dropping onto the hammock below hers.

Oh, no!

She blinked hard and twisted her head to stare at the bottom hammock before shuddering with relief. Abandoned. Matt was evidently already up and dressed.

Thank heavens. At least he hadn't witnessed her utter and complete humiliation. Now, if she could just...

'I didn't realize you were part bat. Although you did mention having an aversion to the sun yesterday.'

Stevie froze. The words, murmured in a low voice that flowed through her like dark fragrant honey, could only come from one man.

She slowly tilted her head further back and, through the veil of her mosquito net, saw Matt. Upside down, but showered and fresh, while she was...well...

'I had a slight accident.'

One side of his mouth quirked up. Or was it down? She couldn't tell any more. 'Yes, I can see that.'

'Instead of standing there, staring, maybe you could help me figure out how to get down?'

'I kind of like you the way you are.'

'Hey!' Her hair swung below her like a tangled skein of yarn, the lank strands almost brushing the lower hammock. 'Stop fooling around and get over here. I'm starting to get dizzy. I don't think you want a puddle of whatever's left in my stomach all over your bed.'

That did it. In a flash, he'd ducked beneath the netting and was at her side. Two strong arms came out and settled under her shoulders and buttocks. 'Okay, I've got you. Let go.'

'Are you sure?'

He laughed. 'Do you want to do this by yourself?'

The hard floor stared at her from a quite a distance away. Nope, she didn't. She unhooked her legs first and felt the bulge of Matt's biceps as he took the weight of her lower half. When she was certain he wouldn't send her careening to the ground, she unfisted her hands.

And wound up right side up, in his arms. With her face way too close to his neck for comfort.

And the scent she'd caught yesterday as she'd passed him in the hallway?

Heavens, it was still there, headier than ever. Against her better judgement, she closed her eyes and leaned just a bit closer, allowing the air around him to fill her senses. Breathe, exhale, repeat…just like the shampoo commercials advised.

'Better?'

She froze, her lungs ceasing all covert activity. Had she really been sniffing a strange man's neck?

'W-what?'

'Your dizziness. I don't want to set you down if you're going to collapse on me.'

'Oh. Um, no. I think I'm okay.' Her voice came out shakier than she'd hoped, and she wondered if she might fall in a heap after all.

Seemingly oblivious to her confusion, he craned his head to the side and looked at her, making no move to put her down. 'I see we should've reviewed the hammock safety video. If I had actually been in that bed and you'd dropped on top of me, things could have gotten rather ugly.'

No kidding. Especially since her T-shirt had been hiked to kingdom come as she'd dangled there. She glanced down, horrified to find a huge swath of her belly still exposed.

Keep talking, and he won't notice. 'No one mentioned that particular hazard when I applied for the job.'

A muscle twitched in his jaw for a moment or two and she realized how her words must have sounded. Especially when he pivoted away from the pair of hammocks and set her on her feet.

She yanked her Mets T-shirt down over her jogging shorts.

'Not that I'm saying landing on top of you would be hazardous or anything...'

Oh, yes, it would be. Even saying it out loud did wonky things to her breathing which, in turn, had nothing to do with nearly falling out of her hammock.

Thankfully, Tiago appeared behind her, saving her from having to explain her meaning.

'Nilson has breakfast ready, if you're hungry,' he said in Portuguese.

The man shifted from foot to foot as if embarrassed about something. Stevie wondered if he'd seen Matt holding her. Or if he understood enough English to know what they'd been saying.

'*Obrigada*,' Matt said, taking a step back.

'Where do you want me to put your blanket and netting from last night?' Tiago added.

Stevie glanced at the thin barrier surrounding the two hammocks. She would have thought they stayed in place at all times. What if someone wanted to nap? 'Do you normally store this during the day?' She moved the netting to the side and secured it with the bungee cord the way she'd seen it yesterday.

'No.' Color stained Matt's neck, and the word came out half-strangled.

Had she done something worse than hanging upside down from her hammock last night?

Tiago shook his head. 'No, not this net, the one from the deck, where he slept.'

'You...' Stevie's mind tried to work through what the man was saying. 'You didn't sleep here last night?'

'Mateus said it was too hot.'

The fiery color moved from Matt's neck to the tips of his ears. 'What I said was it was cooler out there.' He jabbed a thumb in the direction of the deck before turning away. 'Let's get that breakfast you mentioned.'

As he moved out of the room, Stevie wondered why he'd let her believe that he'd slept below her the whole night when obviously he hadn't. He'd even talked about what a disaster it would have been if she'd fallen on top of him, all the while knowing it hadn't been a remote possibility.

Had it all been an act? Or had he simply woken up to a stuffy room and moved his bed onto the deck?

Except Tiago's shifting seemed to indicate what he'd done wasn't an everyday occurrence. Which implied he normally stayed in his room.

All night.

Stevie stopped off at the restroom to dress and wash her hands and face the best she could. When she finally made it to the dining area, she'd halfway composed herself.

She filled the plate Nilson gave her and found Matt already sitting at the picnic-style table. Dropping onto the bench across from him, she set the food in front of her. 'You know, I can sleep on deck if you're uncomfortable sharing the room with me.'

'I told you why I moved. Besides, it's not good for Tiago and Nilson to have to worry about tiptoeing around during the night.' He glanced down at his plate. 'Or finding a half-dressed woman on deck. I'd prefer you sleep in the bedroom.'

He had a point. But it didn't seem fair to have kicked him out of his own bed. She glanced at the small eating space. 'How about this, then? We can string your hammock up in here before you go to bed and then stow it in the mornings.'

Tiago, who'd evidently been listening in on their conversation—putting paid to her hope that he didn't understand English—chimed in, 'This is a good idea, Mateus. I will install some strong hooks in the wall and center beam…and one in the ceiling for the mosquito net you insist on everyone using.' He paused, fiddling with his fingers. 'Although I understand now why it is so important.'

Matt nodded, a shadow passing through his eyes before he switched over to Portuguese. 'Thank you, my friend.'

Turning his attention to Nilson, he asked, 'How long before we reach the village?'

'We should arrive sometime before dinner.'

'Good. I'd like to go over the charts with you and decide our schedule for the next couple of weeks.' He glanced at Stevie.

TINA BECKETT 43

'Can you fend for yourself for a little while? We'll still need to discuss our...story before we reach the village, though.'

She tensed. Their story. How could she have forgotten about that? She forced a smile to her lips, wondering what he had in mind. 'Don't worry about me, I'll be fine. Shall we meet back here in, say, three hours?'

'That sounds good.'

Three hours. Just enough time to focus some of her nervous energy on something other than the situation at hand.

Stevie ran a forearm over her damp brow, the piece of fine-gauge steel wool gripped between her fingertips.

Okay, boat varnish was a whole lot tougher than the glossy finish on the floors in her apartment in New York.

Which she guessed was a good thing, since the stuff was holding up nicely, despite being pitted and dark with grime. She'd hoped her scrubbing would take off the dirt and leave the finish intact. And that's exactly what was happening.

And that nervous energy she'd been worried about?

Gone. Washed away by rivers of sweat.

Kneeling on a towel to protect her legs from the scorching surface of the deck, Stevie leaned closer to her work area and rubbed at the one-foot section of planking. She paused to adjust her bikini top, admiring the area she'd just cleaned. It might take for ever, but hidden beneath layers of dirt the wood was a rich, glossy mahogany.

Just like the dark sun-kissed hair of the man she'd be working with. So different than Michael's blond hair and fair skin. The only thing they had in common were their blue eyes. But while Michael's were darker and sparkling with intelligence and determination, she hadn't noticed the flecks of cruelty that lay just below the surface until it had been too late. In one careless blow, he'd destroyed their future together, and then, when she'd dared to call him on it, reached out in a rage and crushed her dreams as well. It had only taken one phone call to a few key board members, and she'd been as good as finished.

She shuddered. Michael's eyes were definitely not her favorite feature. Not any more.

Matt's, on the other hand, seemed… She searched for the right word.

Haunted.

She scrubbed harder, forcing her fingers to the task. Why was she even comparing the two men?

A bead of moisture dripped into her eye, and she shook her head, as much to rid herself of any stray thought as to relieve the burning. She settled for blotting it on her bare shoulder, wishing she'd scrounged up a second towel to wipe her face. At this rate, her huge bottle of sunblock wouldn't even last a full day. She peered at the large area of deck behind her.

Three feet down. Thirty or so more to go.

She groaned aloud and pulled the brim of her baseball cap further down her forehead, thankful for the slight shade it provided, and went back to work. It couldn't be easy, keeping up a boat while tending to patients—and she had a feeling money was tight on the hospital ship. But surely someone could have tried to do something for the poor thing. It seemed weary of life in general.

It's not a living thing, Stevie. It's just a boat.

Maybe Michael was right when he'd poked fun of the *Projeto Vida* article. Maybe coming here had been crazy on more than one count, but she hadn't been able to just stay in New York and watch him run her reputation into the—

'You don't have to do that.'

The steel wool went spinning out of her hand, and she scrabbled for it, almost doing a face plant onto the deck. Glancing over her shoulder, she caught Matt standing just behind her, a pair of khaki shorts and grey shirt covering his powerful frame. Tanned feet, the lightest smattering of dark hair visible on top, were shoved into a pair of beige flip-flops.

She sat up in a rush, praying her top was still glued to the right spots. 'I thought we're agreed to meet in three hours.'

'Someone tattled on you, and I had to come see for myself.'

His brows went up, his glance trailing over her. 'So this is what a vascular surgeon looks like when swabbing the decks.'

She stood, all too aware of how grubby she must look in comparison to Matt's neatly groomed appearance. 'It takes quite a bit of talent, evidently, since no one here seems to have mastered the technique.'

He laughed and wagged a finger. 'Not nice.' Holding up a glass of water, the ice tinkled against the sides before he tilted it and took a long swig of the contents. 'Too bad, because I was just bringing you something cool to drink.'

She licked her lips, all thoughts of Michael sliding away as she stared at the condensation collecting on the icy surface of the glass. 'That's just mean.'

'And you're turning pink. I thought vampires hated the sun.' He blinked, his eyes zeroing in on her midriff region, then a frown appeared.

For once, she prayed her color really was due to the heat and not from standing in front of him half-dressed. But she'd expected to be able to run back to the room and change long before she was due to meet him. At least she'd opted for white shorts rather than her bikini bottoms.

'I do…I mean, they do. I've slathered on a ton of sunscreen.'

Handing her the glass, he picked up the bottle of sunblock propped on one of the redwood deck chairs and examined the label. 'You'll need something stronger than this. We're close to the equator.'

She gulped down a couple swallows of water, almost moaning as the icy liquid hit her parched throat. She couldn't resist holding the cold glass to her cheek. 'It's the same stuff I always use, but I guess you're right. It never dawned on me that it would be so hot here.'

'Like I said earlier, you can't learn everything about a place from books.' He glanced at her middle one more time before his eyes came back up and met hers. 'Why don't you go shower the dust off and change before we talk about what needs to happen once we reach the village? Tiago has an aloe plant in the back section of the boat that he keeps on hand for burns. I'll have him cut a piece for you.'

She took another drink. 'Thanks.'

Matt walked over to the area she'd cleaned, and his expression softened. 'I'd forgotten how nice the woodwork is on the boat. It's been a long time since anyone's...' His jaw firmed. 'But I don't expect you to do manual labor while you're here.'

'I want to pull my weight.'

'Don't worry, you'll be pulling your weight and a whole lot more, once we reach shore.'

CHAPTER FIVE

'OKAY. That sounds reasonable.'

Reasonable? That's all she had to say about his crazy idea?

Matt narrowed his eyes and leaned forward in the deck chair. He'd exhausted every other possibility before finally resigning himself to the inevitable: they had to pretend to be husband and wife.

But only if someone asked. And only until he could find a replacement for her.

He'd blurted the words as soon as she'd returned from changing her clothes, half expecting her to demand to be returned to the airport. 'Are you sure you're okay with this?'

'Is there another option?' Dressed in narrow khaki capris and an orange T-shirt, she sipped at a glass of water, seemingly more at ease with the situation than he was...and it was *his* damn idea.

'I haven't been able to come up with anything else.'

'What if I told people I was married—to someone else?'

'It would still raise eyebrows with some. They'd wonder what you were doing here in Brazil without your husband.'

Her lips tightened. 'They'd assume I was messing around behind his back, in other words.'

'Yes.'

'That's irony for you.'

'Excuse me?'

'Nothing. It's not like we're going to send out wedding announcements to all the villages or anything.' She sighed. 'You

said we'd give as few details as possible and only if someone
challenges the story.'

'Well, yes, but—'

'Listen, I know having a woman as part of your team wasn't
what you wanted. You've made that abundantly clear. And now
you're stuck with me. I get it.' She shut her eyes for a minute before reopening them and looking out over the deck. 'Let's just
get through this one village at a time. Maybe the subject will
never come up. If it does, just tell them whatever you want, and
I'll follow your lead.'

Well, that was one way to make him feel like a royal ass.

He took a deep breath and touched her shoulder to bring her
attention back to him. 'None of this is your fault. You thought
you'd be traveling with Tracy, and I thought I'd be traveling down
the river with a man. And you know what? Most of the male doctors I've worked with have bailed before the end of their first
two-week run.' He smiled and searched for something nice to
say. 'Be the one who makes it all the way, okay?'

Stevie's eyes moistened, and she nodded with a solemnity
that made his chest tighten. 'I'm not going anywhere.'

The first village was nothing like she expected.

Kicking off her flip-flops, she took Matt's hand and stepped
out of the dinghy they'd used to reach shore, her feet sinking
into the silt just below water's surface. The slow current swirled
around her toes and ankles, feeling deliciously cool after a morning spent working on the hot deck.

Matt squeezed her hand and released it. 'You ready for this?'

Not really, but, then, she hadn't been ready for anything that
had happened recently. 'We'll soon find out, won't we?'

'Why don't you wait on shore while I gather a few things?' As
if he sensed her sudden case of nerves, he smiled. 'I'll be right
behind you.'

Wading just beyond the reach of the water, she shoved her feet
back into her thong sandals and unrolled her pants legs while
surveying her surroundings.

Wow.

Instead of a haphazard scattering of huts, the mud-bricked structures that lay a short distance ahead were arranged in a neat circle, each door facing a central clearing. A thin layer of smoke rose from a single fire pit. She didn't see anyone at the moment, but the sandy dirt around each dwelling could have come straight from a movie set, with pristine, parallel tracks— like those made from a rake—carving shallow furrows in the soil. Curving to and fro, the grooves flowed around whatever object they encountered, much like the river had drifted around her feet moments earlier.

Stevie breathed deeply, the musty scent of the river mixing with that of ancient vegetation.

It was so quiet here. Peaceful. So different from the turmoil that had ruled her life for the past month.

Even the fierce heat seemed to dissipate, wicked up and away by a canopy of towering trees. She smiled, suddenly glad she'd come.

She turned to see if Matt was as affected as she was, only to jump a mile in the air when a scream pierced the serenity around them. Wheeling toward the sound, expecting to see blood—and lots of it—she saw, instead, a toddler hurrying toward them as fast as her tiny legs would carry her.

That single high-pitched sound soon set off a chain reaction, and answering shrieks went up from every corner of the village. A few seconds later, about fifteen children of all sizes came at them in a mob, their feet obliterating some of the lines in the carefully groomed dirt. Stevie braced herself for impact, only to have them ignore her completely as they encircled Matt, who'd finally reached her side.

What in the world...?

He set his medical bag on the ground beside him and retrieved a large backpack he'd slung over his shoulder. Throwing the children a sly smile, he rooted around inside the bag for a minute or two before pulling out a handful of brightly colored...worms.

Gummy worms.

The things spilled between his fingers, the long strands seeming to take on a life of their own. Several kids screamed in horrified delight, while Stevie stared, hardly believing this was the same man who'd met her with a scowl at the airport a day ago and basically told her to go home. By now, several adults were headed their way, apparently unconcerned with the chaos Matt and Stevie's presence had caused.

'Here, hold these for a minute.' He held the tangled knot of worms toward her, and she crinkled her nose in disgust but allowed him to dump the jellied creatures into her cupped palms.

She swallowed. *They're not real worms. Not real.*

Even as she forced the thought to sweep through her mind, she swore she could feel one or two of them slither along her skin, trying to escape. It was everything she could do not to drop the entire bunch on the ground.

Lifting a brow as if he knew exactly what she was thinking, he gave her a quick grin. 'So, you never back down from a challenge, eh? Let's see if you can handle this one.'

He plucked a green worm from the bunch and held it up by the tail, making it dance a time or two before tilting his head back and opening his mouth. Without a word he dropped the creature inside—whole—then swallowed it. He rubbed his stomach, making fake groaning sounds of pleasure, while she could feel herself turning as green as the worm had once been. The children had evidently been through this routine before and knew it was all a game, because they laughed and began pushing to get a little bit closer.

Matt held up a finger. *'Espera aí. A doutora vai comer a próxima minhoca, não é?'*

No. Absolutely not. She was not going to eat a worm—candied or not.

But when a couple of children began to stomp out a rhythm with their feet—*left-left-right...left-left-right*—and one by one the rest joined in, huge smiles wreathing their faces, she knew she was stuck.

But, oh, she was going to make the man pay. Somehow.

She handed the worms back to Matt and selected the smallest one she could find—which still appeared huge. Closing her eyes, she bit down on its midsection, but the thing was tougher than she expected. Her teeth didn't sever it. She ended up having to slurp it up like a piece of overcooked spaghetti. Her groan, unlike Matt's, wasn't fake—or filled with pleasure—but at least the tart flavor allowed her to pretend the candy was the benign bear-shaped gummies she'd loved as a child.

When she chanced a look at him, a gloating comment on the tip of her tongue, the words died. His attention was focused on her mouth and not on the kids' reaction.

What? Did she have sugar stuck there?

She scrubbed her tongue across her lower lip, a sticky spot of sweetness attesting to the fact that's exactly what had happened.

Clearing his throat, and turning away, he addressed the children. 'So…who's next?'

Hands shot into the air. That was everyone…except for one little girl off to the side. Her hands were hidden behind her back, and she stared at the ground. Stevie elbowed Matt to get his attention, leaning her head in the girl's direction in silent question.

'She lost her mother a month ago to malaria.' Matt's low words were for her ears only.

Shock washed over her. 'Who's taking care of her, then?'

'Everyone, probably. They share responsibility, since most people in the tribe are related in some way or other.' The rest of the children pressed even closer. 'Want to help me divvy these up?'

'You start, I'll help in a minute.' She took one of the worms from his hand—the only pink one she could find—and went over to the girl. Kneeling in front of her, she prayed she could make herself understood despite her accent. 'Look, I chose the prettiest one for you. Would you like to try it?'

Large brown eyes met hers. 'But you didn't like it.'

'Of course I did. I just don't like to eat real *minhocas.*' She gave a mock shudder.

A small smile came to the child's lips. 'You ate a real worm before?'

'Well, no…but I'm pretty sure I wouldn't like it if I did.'

'Me neither.'

'Ma—er, Mr. Matt hasn't brought these little guys here before?' She touched the worm with her finger, glad she'd washed her hands before coming ashore. Then she rolled her eyes at the automatic need to clean everything in sight. Being a doctor, she knew it came with the territory. But she was in a different world now. With a completely different set of rules. She needed to watch Matt and follow his lead. The girl shook her head. 'He brought little bears the last time he came.'

Stevie laughed. 'The bears are my favorites! These taste just like them, though. Even if they do look a little less appetizing.' She held the worm closer. 'Wanna try?'

The shrug that followed appeared disinterested, but Stevie could swear a glimmer of curiosity lurked behind her eyes.

'My name's Stevie. What's yours?'

'Madelena.'

'That's a very nice name.' She glanced at Matt, who was still distributing the candy. Surprise again washed over her when his deep chuckle rose above the noise.

He truly loved what he did. It showed in the sparkle of his eyes, the ready smile that appeared whenever he addressed the kids, and most of all in that delicious laugh.

She turned back to the girl. 'How about if I sneak another worm and eat one with you? Would that be all right?'

A quick nod. 'You're not afraid?'

Something behind the words made her insides clench. This child had probably faced fears she herself could not even imagine. Not the least of which was losing someone she loved.

'No. Not of a candy worm.' She brushed a piece of the girl's straight dark hair away from her face. 'But I'm scared of plenty of other things. Let me get a worm, and I'll be right back.'

She stood on the fringe of the children surrounding Matt and waved at him. 'Can you spare another worm?'

At first she thought her words had been swallowed by the ruckus around him, but he made his way over and held out his hand, letting her choose.

'Thank you,' he said.

She picked up one of the worms and tried to ignore the way her fingertips sizzled when they connected with his skin. 'For what?'

'Caring.'

And with that single word, he returned to the other children, leaving Stevie to stare after him.

She shook herself and went back to Madelena. Handing the little girl the pink candy, she took the sickly yellow-green one for herself. 'Ready?'

'Ready.' Madelena cocked her head, another smile coming to her face at the way the candy quivered as she held it in the air.

They both downed their worms, their eyes meeting. Then they burst out laughing.

'Good?'

'Yes.' The child looked longingly at Matt.

Stevie stood. 'Go ahead. I'm sure he'll give you another one.'

The girl darted away and joined the other kids. Matt immediately noticed and drew her close to his side, sneaking another piece of candy into her hands. He glanced in Stevie's direction for a second and something like warm satisfaction flitted across his face before he went back to dealing with the children.

With all the worms devoured and the kids off doing other things, she helped Matt lug ashore a wooden fruit crate filled with health packets he'd brought for the adults, most of whom still lingered nearby as if knowing the drill.

She picked up one of the small sealed packages and looked at it curiously. 'What're in these?'

'Basic first-aid items, along with water purification tablets and condoms.'

'Condoms. Really? Do they use them?'

He shrugged. 'Who knows? We try to educate them in the hows and whys, but the rest is up to them. Along with the normal STDs, there've been several outbreaks of Lábrea fever in the neighboring villages. Condom use is one avenue of prevention.'

'I've never heard of Lábrea fever.'

'It's basically a co-infection of Hepatitis B and D. Very lethal.

We try to vaccinate newborns against Hep B, but since we're not present for most live births, it can be hit and miss.' He smiled at the adults and motioned them over. 'By bundling the condoms with the rest of the first-aid items, it removes any stigma or embarrassment and presents contraception as a normal part of staying healthy.'

Matt took his time passing out the packets, speaking to each person in line about their family and health. A spark of admiration lit inside her. How on earth did he remember all these names and faces, much less each medical history?

A young lady took a packet, then hesitated. Matt asked her a few questions and then knelt down to examine a couple of swollen bites on her foot.

He pulled on a pair of surgical gloves, glancing at Stevie as he did. 'Can you finish distributing the kits while I deal with this?'

'Sure. What's wrong with her?'

'She has botfly larvae.'

Stevie crinkled her nose. 'Oh.'

'Not afraid of a couple of worms, are you?'

'The gummy variety are looking better and better.'

By the time the line of people had dwindled to nothing, most of the packets were gone. She gathered the few remaining kits and went over to where Matt and the woman sat on some stools, chatting like old friends.

Matt looked up and nodded at the packets in her arms. 'How many are left?'

'About ten.'

His brows rose. 'Good. Every trip the response gets better. We may run out of supplies before we reach the last village but, if so, we can cut our trip short and go back to Coari for more.'

'Sounds good.' Stevie sat on a third stool and smiled at their patient. '*Tudo bem?* How's your foot?'

'It will soon be well.'

Peering down at the three red welts on the upper portion of the woman's instep, she noticed a thick layer of goop covering each spot. 'What did you put on them?'

'Vaseline. It cuts off the larvae's air supply and will hopefully suffocate the little buggers. If we're lucky, they'll poke their heads out to try to breathe, and we can pull them out with tweezers. If that doesn't work, we'll wait until morning and hope they're dead.'

'Why not just numb the area and cut them out? It would be quicker and more efficient.'

He laughed. 'Spoken like a surgeon. Quicker is not better in this case. She'd be left with three incisions and stitches. If the site's not cared for, you risk infection. Besides, we may not be back in a week to remove the sutures.'

Okay, he had her there. 'So we wait.'

'Yup. I'm sure we'll have other patients in the meantime.'

He was right. By nightfall, they'd seen at least twenty people with a variety of minor ailments, while the woman with the botfly larvae waited for the Vaseline to work its magic.

Exhaustion rolled over her.

How had Matt handled this kind of caseload alone?

Tracy was right. He needed another doctor on the team…and Stevie intended to make sure she was a help, not a hindrance.

Matt switched on a large battery-powered lantern once dusk hit, and its strong glow chased away the darkness. Combined with the light from several cooking fires behind them, she could almost believe it was still day, if not for the dark sky stretching out above them—and the accompanying heaviness of her eyelids.

'Do you want to go back to the boat?' he asked. 'I'm going to take one more shot at removing our little friends.'

'I'll help. Just tell me what to do.'

'You sure? You look a little worse for wear.'

'Gee, thanks.'

He shook his head. 'I didn't mean it that way. It's late. You must be tired.'

'No more than you. I'm here to help, remember?'

'Okay.' He removed a pair of tweezers from their protective packaging and propped the woman's foot on his knee, giving her shoulder a comforting pat. 'Are you ready?' he asked her.

The woman nodded, stifling a yawn.

He glanced at Stevie. 'Here's what we're going to do. You squeeze each site with steady pressure, while I try to get a hold of the larva and pull it out. Some doctors are using venom extractors nowadays, but I've found the old-fashioned way works best.'

Stevie took a deep breath. 'I'm ready whenever you are.'

The removals went without a hitch, although Stevie's stomach twisted a little at times. Their patient, on the other hand, seemed to take everything in her stride, watching the process with interest.

Matt grinned. 'Well, that was easy.'

Easy? *Easy?*

He chuckled and went about wiping the bites with an alcohol-soaked pad, telling their patient to keep the site clean until it healed.

Before leaving, the woman took both of Stevie's hands in hers and gave her a light kiss on the cheek.

'Thank you for today,' she said. 'Madelena is my sister's child, and she is still very sad. I saw what you did for her. Her smile lit up my heart.'

Stevie nodded and tried to respond, but the words wouldn't make it past the lump in her throat. So she squeezed the woman's hands, then stared after her as she walked toward the circle of huts.

'I think we'll call it a night.' Matt's quiet voice brought her attention back to him.

Clearing her voice, she said, 'I agree. It's been a long day.'

She held out her hand, offering to help him up from the stool. He hesitated, then allowed her to haul him to his feet. Instead of releasing her immediately, his fingers curled around hers, the palm-to-palm contact sending shockwaves rippling across her skin.

'You did good today,' he said.

'Sorry about looking queasy the way I did. I just didn't expect the things to look quite so disgusting.'

'I'm not talking about the botflies.'

'Then what? I—I didn't do much of anything.'

'You did. You let them touch you.'

Puzzled, she shook her head. 'So did you.'

'No, I don't mean they touched you like this.' His thumb strummed across her knuckles, the friction from the calloused pad sending a shiver over her. He released her and put his hand to his chest. 'You let them touch you here.'

She'd touched more than just the villagers.

And over the next two days Matt took pains to avoid any physical contact with Stevie, even by accident. Because while he'd complimented her for opening her heart to the people they worked with, holding her hand had almost caused him to open a part of himself as well.

And that couldn't happen.

She seemed to be adjusting remarkably well, but he had to remember she was still in the 'tourist' phase of her visit. The honeymoon period when everything about Brazil was new and fascinating. That would wear off soon enough. Then culture shock would set in. Fascination would turn to irritation, and irritation would change to something far worse.

The day-to-day drudgery had worn every other doctor down. Each had walked up the gangway full of hope and good will. They'd left, simmering with frustration and resentment. For all he knew, Stevie would follow suit. She'd scoot out of the Amazon just as fast as she could.

If she did, the next time Tracy hired someone, Matt would make sure she stuck to their bargain.

Men only.

Seeing Stevie in that white bikini top the other day had reaffirmed that policy. It had also caused him to lie awake in his hammock for hours every night. When he did manage to sleep, the dreams…

It was no wonder he was exhausted.

He closed his eyes, trying *not* to see her swivel towards him in slow motion as she rose from the deck, her sleek blonde ponytail swinging from the back of the baseball cap, a dusty handprint stamped across the pale bare skin of her stomach. It didn't work. Every freckle on her shoulders, every luscious curve of her body was forever tattooed onto his brain. He'd wanted to take the steel wool from her hands and...

'Oh, my!' Stevie's voice came from behind him, throwing a bucket of cold water over his thoughts, dashing them away and hopefully taking care of the growing problem behind his zipper.

She continued to speak, having no idea she'd just been the object of some pretty explicit inner commentary. 'I can't believe what you've done.'

He glanced at the newly scrubbed deck, praying to God that's what she was talking about. 'Nilson did most of it, I just finished it off.'

'When? It wasn't like this when I went to bed last night.'

No, and he couldn't very well tell her *she* was the cause of his working late into the night. Again.

'Tiago and Nilson wanted to surprise you.'

She smiled. 'Well, it worked. It's gorgeous.'

She was right. The neglected woodwork gleamed from their efforts. A sense of shame swept through Matt. It was almost like he'd been punishing the boat for what had happened to Vickie. Or, maybe, like his life...he simply hadn't cared enough to make the effort once she'd died.

So why now?

Guilt for Stevie taking on the job herself?

Or was it more than that?

Squatting down, Stevie ran her fingers across the rich wood. 'Where did you get the varnish? I couldn't find any when I looked in the storage room.'

'It's boiled linseed oil. The stuff has been around for ages. I wasn't sure it was still good, but Nilson tried it on a small area and it came out great.'

'I'll say. I honestly thought it was some kind of commercial finish. It's just so...' She glanced up at him, her teeth worrying the lower left corner of her lip. 'It really means a lot to me that you did this. I'll have to thank the guys.'

She stood. 'Oh, I found some lemons in the fruit bin and made some lemonade, I hope you don't mind. I brought you a glass.'

'Of course I don't mind. The supplies belong to all of us.' He spied the bamboo tray on the table between the two lounge chairs, a wedge of lemon jammed onto the side of each glass.

Why hadn't he heard her come up?

Easy, he'd been too busy trying not to mentally undress her. He glanced at her clothes. At least she was fully covered in a lime green T-shirt and pants that came to mid-calf. Her hair, wet from a recent shower, was scraped back in a high ponytail. She looked clean scrubbed and cool.

And totally kissable.

He was insane. That had to be it. River fever.

He followed her to the seating area and before dropping into the nearest chair he swabbed the sweat from his face and neck the best he could with a nearby rag, the perspiration having little to do with work and everything to do with the woman standing in front of him.

'Smart.' She nodded at the piece of cloth. 'I ended up wiping the sweat with my hands and found filthy handprints all over myself later.'

Yes. He remembered. And he'd been tempted to add a few dirty handprints of his own.

She sat in the other chair and handed him a glass. 'Drink it while it's cold.'

Careful not to touch her fingers, he took the glass, then downed a third of the drink in one gulp. The tart liquid did the trick, cooling him in an instant. Sighing, he stretched his legs out in front of him. 'I can't remember the last time I had lemonade.'

It had probably been with Vickie, but that seemed ages ago now. He tried to dredge up the memory of them sitting on the deck like this. A sliver of panic went through him when he couldn't remember what they'd talked about the last time life had been normal.

And he preferred not to think of the hours they'd spent rushing back to the nearest city, trying to reach a hospital in time.

Cool fingers slid across his wrist. 'Are you okay?'

He moved his hand, but not before the touch he'd frantically been avoiding did some lasting damage. To cover his brusque withdrawal, he dragged his fingers through his hair, hoping the light wind blowing across the bow had ruffled it enough to give him a valid excuse. 'I'm fine. Just enjoying the quiet.'

Agonizing in the quiet was more like it.

Only when she picked up her glass of lemonade, her knuckles white as she carefully sipped from it, staring out at the river, did he realize how his words might have come across. 'Listen, I didn't mean you were talking too much. You're not. I just have a lot on my mind right now.'

That was the understatement of the century.

'It's fine. I actually just came up to bring you some lemonade and to ask how long until we reach the next village.' She stood, her half-empty glass still in her hand. 'I'll get out of your hair.'

Something in her face—*hurt, maybe?*—made him reach out and do exactly what he'd sworn not to do: touch her…his fingers connecting with hers for a second. 'Don't go. We've still got a couple of hours before we reach our next stop.' His jaw clenched for a second, wishing he could swallow the request. He settled for qualifying it. 'If you've got something else to do, though…'

She studied him for a minute, then the tense lines around her mouth relaxed into a smile that cut right through the defenses he'd erected over the last couple of days. 'Are you sure you don't mind?'

'I'm sure. It's nice having someone to enjoy the view with.' He lifted his lemonade. 'And thanks for this.'

'You're welcome.' She lowered herself back in the chair and looked at the water. 'It is beautiful here.'

'It can be.' He took in the trees hanging over the river bank, heard the ordinary sounds of the jungle. On the surface, he supposed she was right. But underneath… 'The Amazon can also be cruel. Unforgiving.'

'I imagine it can be.' Stevie propped her chin on the backs of her laced fingers, silent for a moment, then turned toward him.

'I really do want to help. Give me some time to prove I'm up to the task, okay?'

'And if you're not?' Matt knew he was the one with the problem. But what could he do? He'd mentioned enjoying the scenery a minute or so ago. Unfortunately, the scenery included a whole lot more than the river beneath the boat. And right now Stevie was high on that list of local attractions.

She shrugged. 'If I'm not, I'll be the first one to admit it.'

'Will you?'

'Yes.' Her green eyes held his for several long seconds. Matt's chest tightened as he met her steady gaze. He struggled to keep his attention centered, but the quick moistening of her lips tossed his good intentions right over the side of the boat, where he swore they hit the water with an audible *splash*.

His body went on full alert, and he realized a few seconds too late that when she'd shifted to the right, he'd mirrored her movement and wound up way too close. If not separated by the small table, their shoulders would have bumped.

Lean back toward center. Now.

Despite the command, his body stayed right where it was.

'Matt…I need to tell you something.'

The words were so quiet he gave up trying to move, angling his head to hear her. As he did, the scent of the lemons she'd squeezed—and something uniquely feminine—rose to tease his nostrils.

'Okay.'

Why the hell was he whispering all of a sudden?

He cleared his throat. 'What is it?'

Her tongue skidded across her lips again and disappeared. 'I wanted to tell you that I know about—'

Tiago appeared in the doorway, the worried grooves on either side of his mouth slicing through the cozy atmosphere like a guillotine.

Matt stood. 'What's wrong?'

The other man twisted his hands in front of him, his mouth opening then snapping shut. He took a deep breath and tried again. 'Miss Tracy's on the radio. There's an outbreak in one of the villages.'

Tiago paused for several long seconds, and Matt saw the truth written on the other man's face even before his next words registered. 'Mateus, it's dengue fever.'

CHAPTER SIX

'WHICH village?' Matt held the microphone to his mouth, his other hand gripping the wheel. He wasn't steering the boat since Nilson had cut the engine the moment Matt had entered the room, but he'd needed something solid to hold onto.

His crewmembers stared at him from across the bridge, their faces twin masks of dismay. Tiago had even crossed himself the second Matt had reached for the radio.

'Tupari.' Tracy's voice came across the airwaves, the crackle of static making it hard to understand what she said.

Matt swore softly. 'It'll take me a day and a half to get there.'

'How serious is it?' The question came from Stevie, who stood to his right.

He held up a finger, signaling her to wait.

Tracy's garbled answer came back. 'I know. And unfortunately, by the...you arrive the rest...village will have been exposed.'

'I realize that.' His eyes closed for a minute, tension grabbing him by the throat and threatening to slowly squeeze the life from him. He knew he'd eventually have to face a dengue epidemic again, knew that it had been far too long since the last outbreak. But recognizing his fears and confronting them were two different things.

'Do you...me to come down for this one?'

His glance clipped Stevie's before looking away. Her presence made an already difficult situation unbearable. 'No, even if you could get a direct flight out of São Paulo, we don't have time to go back to Coari and pick you up.' He paused. 'Did you have a chance to do any more looking?'

'I'm having trouble hearing…say again…chance to…?'

He sighed. 'Never mind.'

'Matt, douse yourselves…repellent before you get anywhere near that place. You'll…no use to anyone if you contract dengue again.'

Despite the interference on the line, he understood exactly what she was getting at. Once you'd acquired one strain of dengue, you were immune to it, but there were still three other types waiting in the wings. And, worse, the sufferer's antibodies tended to play a nasty trick with the next infection, unwittingly helping it gain a foothold. If that happened, the virus could escalate into the deadly hemorrhagic form.

He swallowed. She hadn't mentioned what had happened to Vickie. There was no need. He and his wife had both been young, naïve and stupidly certain of their own immortality. How wrong they'd been.

'I'll be careful.'

'Do. And, Matt…sure to check in when you get there.'

'Will do. Over.' He ended the transmission and slid the mouthpiece back into its holder, fiddling with it for a second or two. Anything to give himself time to wrench his mind away from the horrors of the past. Of racing to the nearest hospital, which was a day away, only to be told it was too late. His wife's organs were shutting down, bleeding from countless spots inside her. And their baby…

'What's going on?' Stevie's voice did what he couldn't do on his own: pulled him back to the present.

'There's an outbreak of dengue fever in one of the villages.'

'I heard that part.'

'It's mosquito borne, which means we'll need those nets you brought.'

She nodded. 'Will a hundred and fifty be enough?'

'They'll have to be.' He glanced to the side, realizing Nilson and Tiago were hanging on his every word, even though he'd been speaking in English. He turned back to Stevie. It was too late to take her back now. Besides, she'd fight him tooth and nail if he even tried. The best he could hope to do was protect her from exposure. He swallowed. 'You wanted a chance to prove you could do the job? You've got it.'

Her chin went up. 'I'm ready.'

'Good, but I won't tolerate anyone taking unnecessary risks.'

'Understood. Listen…I, uh, studied dengue briefly in medical school, but it's been a while. You've seen cases firsthand. Can you fill me in?'

Perfect.

Even as his teeth ground together in useless frustration, he knew she wasn't to blame. A vascular surgeon wouldn't have much cause to keep up with the changing face of tropical medicine. 'I have a desk reference with a whole section on dengue. You'll need to read it and bring yourself up to speed.'

'Is it Manson's reference?'

He nodded. 'You're familiar with it?'

'I have a copy at home that I started reading, but with all the extra luggage I brought, I didn't dare add any more weight. I hadn't reached the section on dengue yet.'

'Like you heard me tell Tracy, it'll take us over a day to reach the village, so you can catch up while we travel. I also have some case files you can read through.'

'Any casualties from this particular outbreak?'

'One child so far. Several others are ill.'

Her arms wrapped around her waist. 'How awful.'

'Remember what I said at the airport about battlefield triage?'

She nodded.

'You're about to experience it firsthand.'

Stevie reached the exam room and pulled the silver chain holding the key from beneath her T-shirt. Fumbling with her mother's wedding ring, which was housed on the same necklace, she tried to separate it from the key. She ended up having to pull the whole thing over her head. Instead of pushing the ring aside, she stared at it for a second before closing her fingers around it and holding it to her mouth.

More precious than the gold it was made from, she kept the simple piece of jewelry next to her heart, like her own personal set of dog tags—the symbol of who she was and where she'd come from. Sighing, she unlocked the door and dropped the chain back over her head.

The light switch should be right… *Click*. Yep, there it was. A low-hanging ceiling fan came on in conjunction with the bulb, the low *whump, whump* of the rotating blades a soothing cadence that helped calm her jangled nerves.

Why was she so edgy, anyway? Was it because of the outbreak?

No, it had more to do with Matt's reaction to it. And the fact that he'd asked Tracy, 'Are you still looking?'

She could only take that to mean he still wanted to replace her. A lump of hurt that never seemed go away rose in her throat. Michael had certainly had no trouble replacing her with another woman, so why would Matt be any different? He seemed anxious to find another doctor and send her on her way. The faster, the better. The hurt grew until she struggled to breathe past it. Maybe this was how the botflies felt as they slowly suffocated beneath the weight of the Vaseline.

Why didn't Matt want her here? Because of the marriage issue? But they'd resolved that. Or so she'd thought. She could have sworn he'd been softening toward her back at the last village, and then a few minutes ago on deck. But evidently she'd imagined it. All of it.

Her mouth twisted. She wanted to stay, no matter what he thought of her. Her initial reasons for traveling to the Amazon might not have been purely philanthropic, but she'd toyed with the idea of doing this very thing some time in the future—only that future had appeared out of nowhere, landing on her head like a block of granite.

Besides, what was the alternative? Go back to New York? Beg Michael to intercede on her behalf with the hospital's board of directors after what he'd done?

Right.

He was the one who'd written her up in the first place. And

her tentative overtures to a few of the other local hospitals had been met with polite smiles that had ended in silence. No one liked a doctor who refused to play by the rules.

Realizing she'd been staring off into space, she quickly scanned the bookcase until she found *Manson's Tropical Diseases*, its green cover identical to the one she'd left at home. She tugged it from its spot, and found a chair beneath a low Formica desk at the far end of the counter. The enlarged image of an *Aedes Aegypti* mosquito on the cover caught her eye as she sat down. Taking a moment, she studied it. Perched on a vibrant green leaf, the creature's white striped legs and graceful curves gave it a delicate appearance. It was quite beautiful, actually.

Until you looked closer and realized the red abdomen was full of blood from a recent feed.

She shuddered. Looks were deceiving. What seemed harmless on the outside could cause a wealth of misery if you allowed it to venture too close. Because once it achieved contact, it anesthetized you. You wouldn't even know what hit you, until it was too late.

Just like with Michael.

Thumbing through the index, she found dengue…already circled by someone. Her brows went up. Matt had evidently encountered this disease more than once, which made sense, given his reaction to Tracy's call. The nets she'd brought would help, but they were a drop in the bucket compared to the number of people who made their homes along the Amazon River. Unless people were educated in mosquito eradication, they would remain vulnerable.

She started to flip back through the book, but it fell open to the very page she was searching for.

Weird.

Even stranger were the handwritten notes crammed into every available space along the margins. The words caught and held her attention, and she turned the book sideways in an attempt to decipher them.

She couldn't picture Matt having this kind of writing. The small, neat letters were formed with a flowing hand…feminine.

Her teeth came down on her lip.

Matt hadn't scrawled these notes at all. A woman had. And they told a story that made her heart cramp within her chest. As she read further, the notations changed from concise observations to rambling, emotional editorials bulleted with dates. Matt's name appeared periodically along with another name she didn't recognize. The handwriting grew shaky as the days rolled by. A rusty, smudged fingerprint at the top of the next page looked strangely like...

Everything came together in an instant, and tears sprang to her eyes as she stared blindly at the wall.

These notes had been penned by Matt's wife. And they recounted a struggle to the death.

Her death.

From the very disease they were on their way to fight.

CHAPTER SEVEN

'DID you find the information on dengue?' Matt never took his eyes off the river, his hip propped against the deck's railing.

'I finished the chapter.' Should she tell him what she'd found in the process? He must have forgotten the writing in the book's margins, or surely he wouldn't have suggested she read it.

Or had he meant it as a warning, trying to scare her off?

'Good.' His fingers went to the back of his neck and massaged before tilting his head to pop the joints. Something he'd done regularly for the last four days.

The need to relieve the suffering of another—no matter what the personal or professional cost to herself—quickly overcame her feeble argument that this man could hurt her if she got too close.

'Turn around,' she said.

'What?' He twisted to look at her, wincing slightly when his cervical spine rotated past the thirty-degree mark.

'Your neck is bothering you. I studied chiropractic medicine for a while. Did someone diagnose the problem?'

He shrugged. 'I fell off a ladder a while back. Muscles are still a little stiff. It's nothing.'

'If it's nothing, then you won't mind my taking a look, will you?'

She'd been tempted to offer to work on his neck the first time she noticed him in pain, but he'd been unapproachable, and her courage had failed her. And since then even their accidental touches had sent her hormones on a rampage, which made her wary of anything more than momentary contact.

Yet here she was, *asking* to lay her hands on him?

Before she could retract her offer, he turned around and faced the water without a word.

Okay, that was as close to an invitation as she was likely to get.

She moved in a step or two, her head tilting as she tried to figure out where to begin. With the difference in their heights, there was no way she'd be able to do this with him standing up. She glanced around, noting one of the redwood chairs off to the side. The back was low enough to let her access his neck and high enough so she wouldn't have to hunch over while she worked.

Hefting it, her breath hissed out in surprise at how heavy it was. She waddled a few feet, then set it down in the middle of the deck with a slight '*Oomph*'.

He turned at the sound, frowning at the chair. 'Stevie, I really don't think—'

'Then don't.'

'Don't what?'

'Think.' Because she evidently wasn't. 'You're too tall. I need you to sit down.'

Something in her face must have warned him not to argue further because, to her surprise, he did as she'd ordered.

She stood in front of him and raised her brows.

'What?' he asked.

'Shirt.'

'You've got to be kidding me.'

'I'm a doctor. I've seen it all before.' She laughed. 'You know, I've always wanted to say that, but my patients tend to be out cold by the time I get to them.'

'Lucky them.'

She chuckled again. 'Come on, don't be a spoilsport.'

'I'm glad you think this is funny.' Even so, he grabbed the hem of his shirt and yanked it over his head,

Her breath hitched when the firm, tanned skin of his chest

came into view, her stomach doing a couple little back flips in the process.

Okay, this might not have been one of her smartest ideas.

To cover her reaction, she took the shirt from his hands and laid it over the matching chair a few feet away before moving behind him. Unfortunately the view from the back was just as delicious as the front, and she couldn't help but mouth, '*Oh. My. God.*' Just to get the words out of her system.

You've seen it all before, remember?

She rolled her eyes, but went about opening and closed her fingers to limber up the joints and prepare them for the inevitable. There was nothing to do but go through with it now that she'd opened her big mouth.

The first contact with his flesh was every bit as bad as she'd feared, a running jolt of electricity leaping the gap between his skin and her fingertips and racing along her neural highway. Its destination? Well, it certainly wasn't her brain.

Ignore it. You can do this.

Palms flat, she curled her fingers around his nape and massaged with strong firm strokes. She allowed herself a brief rush of pleasure at the heat coming off him, before beating the feeling back and working out a strategy.

A professional one.

She took a deep breath. Okay, once she got his muscles loosened up, she could probe further into the structures of his neck.

Only they didn't loosen. If anything, the flesh beneath her hands tightened even more.

She stopped what she was doing to give his shoulders a quick jiggle. 'Don't tense up on me.'

'I'm not.' The stiff, tight growl belied his words.

'Ha!' She dug the pads of her thumbs into the rigid muscles of his shoulders. 'You think I can't feel that?'

When he winced but said nothing, she shook her head in exasperation. 'We're not leaving here until I see what I'm dealing with. Unless you'd prefer to do this on one of the exam tables.'

His spine turned to stone...her knees to jelly.

Oops.

'I mean, I can't do a whole lot of structural manipulation while you're sitting up. You know…like an adjustment.'

'Were you even licensed?'

She relaxed and grabbed the lifeline he'd unwittingly thrown out. 'Nope. But almost. One man's back did me in. Too much fur.'

Unlike Matt's back, which was warm and smooth, with a nice ripple of muscle just beneath the surface. Except for this one spot on the right-hand side where his neck met his shoulder. Her fingers danced toward it, located the insertion point of the muscle and dug in. Deep.

'*Ow!*'

Stevie laughed. 'Just sit back and enjoy the ride.'

'Enjoy?' His next groan skated the line between pain and pleasure. If she was judging the sound correctly, it tipped slightly toward the pleasure end of the spectrum.

Working the taut muscles for a few more minutes, she made sure she found the sore areas and smoothed them with long brushing strokes of her palms.

She leaned closer. 'Better?'

'No.'

Oh, yes, it was. Because that low word ended on a sigh. 'Give me fifteen minutes, and I'll have you singing a different tune.'

He grunted a negation, but his head tilted slightly to the left, allowing her more access. She kept one step ahead of her hands, not letting them know what was coming next. Because if her hands didn't know, Matt wouldn't. And he couldn't tense himself against the deeper strokes.

'I thought vascular surgeons were supposed to have a light touch.'

'Is that an insult?' She kneaded higher, moving to the spot where the muscles attached to his skull.

'No.' He rolled his shoulders forward and gave a deep sigh. 'Never.'

'Want me to stop?'

'Uh-uh. Not yet.'

'See? That's the way it always plays out in the end. First they cry…then they sigh.'

'Very funny. I thought you said you'd never treated chiropractic patients.'

'No, I said I stopped when I got the *wrong* patient.'

'I think you missed your calling.'

She grinned, still trying to ease the tightness in a particularly stubborn area. 'That's not what you said earlier.'

'I was an idiot earlier.'

'Ha! You need me, whether you want to admit it or not. I'll soon have you begging me to stay.'

Matt had no intention of begging her for anything, even though his flesh was now loose as a goose. Except for one vital part of him, which was quickly becoming an embarrassment.

'I think that's enough for now,' he muttered.

'Are you sure? There's this one spot that I can't quite get to co-operate.'

No kidding. She wasn't the only one. But that spot wasn't going to get any better until she stopped what she was doing. 'Yes. I'm sure.' He cleared his throat and cast around for another subject. 'Tell me about the chapter on dengue.'

Her hands went still, but the coolness of her skin against his made him very aware of the continued contact.

'What do you mean?'

'I mean, did you learn anything new?'

'Matt…I…'

Why was she hesitating?

Hell.

He remembered exactly what was in his Manson's reference. 'You saw the writing.'

She broke contact and came around to the front, squatting in front of him. Her eyes had darkened, the shimmer of tears hovering near the surface. 'Yes.'

Maybe it was for the best. The thought of taking her into the middle of that outbreak made his stomach churn, a sensation that would only get worse the closer they got to Tupari. 'Then you know what we're about to be faced with.'

'I do now.' She took his hand, wrapping both of hers around it. 'I'm sorry.'

He closed his eyes to shut out the compassion on her face, and focused, instead, on the steady grip of her fingers. 'Don't be sorry. Just be ready.'

The shore was crowded, the faces solemn testaments of what Matt knew they'd find.

'Oh, my God,' said Stevie.

He watched her slide her feet into a pair of white flip-flops as Nilson lowered the dinghy over the side of the boat and into the water. The pink polish glinted up at him as a reminder of her first night on the boat. It seemed like ages ago.

Her khaki cargo shorts and T-shirt suddenly took on new meaning. Too much exposed skin. All it would take was just one bite. 'Go put on repellent.'

'I already did, this morning.'

'Do it again. These mosquitoes feed during the day. And with the number of villagers infected, lying in the open...' He swallowed, knowing exactly what might happen. 'There could be a catastrophe. No one gets off this boat without protection.'

'What about you and the rest of the crew?'

'I've already put mine on, and Tiago and Nilson know the drill. You can unpack the nets you brought while you're at it. We're going to need them.'

Her green eyes scanned the shore. 'I brought some citronella candles as well.'

'Good. Bring a couple on deck, put each one in a pan of water, and light them. We'll need all the help we can get.'

She nodded and turned to walk away, but he reached out and wrapped a hand around her wrist, not sure why it was suddenly so important to spend one more minute with her before they went ashore. The soft skin beneath his fingers was already damp with humidity, but she felt warm and alive. Brimming with good health.

For now.

He swallowed. What had he been thinking, bringing her into a situation like this?

A glint of worry passed through her eyes as she peered up at him. 'What is it?'

'Remember what I said. Don't take any chances.'

'I'll try not to.'

When he spotted a canoe being launched into the water with the village chief himself onboard, Matt knew things were bad. Really bad.

He let go of Stevie's arm. 'Go.' He nudged her toward the passageway that led to their quarters. 'And don't come back on deck until you've sprayed yourself from head to toe.'

CHAPTER EIGHT

'SHE has it.'

Stevie already knew the answer, but hearing Matt confirm the diagnosis made her chest ache even more.

They'd been battling the outbreak for the last four days, and even though they'd worked in shifts, she was emotionally and physically exhausted.

'What about her baby?'

His eyes took on a hard edge. 'She's the patient. Concentrate on her.'

In the middle of swabbing the woman's feverish brow, Stevie's hand stopped in mid-stroke. 'How can you say that?'

Matt's attitude since they'd arrived had been unbelievable. No more jokes. No candy. Not even a reassuring word to his patients. He'd handled the ill tribe members with an icy efficiency that made her cringe. She understood why doctors needed to maintain a certain emotional distance, but his lack of compassion went beyond the pale.

He hadn't been like this at the previous village, so it must be a reaction to facing the illness that had taken his wife's life.

Even so, that didn't excuse his—

'If you treat her, you treat the fetus.'

His cool pronouncement interrupted her mental rant. But it didn't stop the metaphorical steam from shooting out her ears in angry waves.

The man standing to the side of the clearing watching them through the opening of the hut pulled her attention from Matt.

He was the same person who'd been in the first canoe after the *Projeto Vida* dropped anchor. His attitude seemed as detached as Matt's, but she sensed an undercurrent of worry running through him, despite the austere, emotionless cut of his face.

'Who's that?' She nodded in the man's direction.

Matt glanced up, taking his stethoscope from the woman's belly, where he'd been listening. 'The woman's father.'

'And her husband? Where is he?'

He shrugged. 'I have no idea. Probably meeting with the medicine man.'

The woman in question shuddered as the fever again racked her body, a moan passing through parched lips. Stevie was seeing firsthand why dengue had earned the nickname break-bone fever. She'd watched person after person shake with chills so violent their teeth rattled in their heads. There'd been one death since their arrival, bringing the total number of victims to two. But a few other patients were critical, including the one they now tended.

Matt's fingers palpated the woman's abdomen. His earlier words said he didn't care, but his actions belied that as he checked the baby's condition. Surely he wanted it to survive as much as she did.

'At least we haven't had any hemorrhagic cases,' she said.

'The village is lucky. This is their first outbreak in recent history. When it strikes again, they won't be so fortunate.' He glanced into her face. 'The baby's fine, by the way. I'll go update her father.'

Stevie sagged in relief as he climbed to his feet and went over to the man. The girl's father was taller than most of the other villagers she'd seen, but Matt still towered over him. Lithe and powerful, her fellow doctor projected authority—from his straight bearing to his hard carved features. The only weakness she'd seen in him had been his stiff neck, which seemed a little better since she'd worked on him. But with the stress he was under, those muscles were going to seize up again, if he wasn't careful.

Remembering the icy intensity of his eyes as he'd gripped her arm and told her to go below and spray herself with repellent sent a shiver over her. The reaction had nothing to do with the fear of illness and everything to do with the heat of his touch.

He leaned down and took something out of his pack before trying to hand it to the girl's father. The man waved it away with a dismissive gesture. What was he doing? Matt's voice rose enough for her to hear it.

'These people will follow your lead. If you won't protect yourself, neither will they, and more people could die.'

Repellent. Matt was trying to get him to take a bottle and use it.

The man glanced at his daughter who lay on the pallet, her head tossing from side to side in agony. Stevie could almost see the wheels turning in his brain. He felt like he'd be betraying his daughter if he did something to keep himself from getting sick while she lay there, both she and her baby in danger.

Stevie finished swabbing the girl's head and ducked beneath the mosquito netting that, while too late to protect the young woman, kept mosquitoes from getting to her and then biting her friends and relatives, thus spreading the illness. She walked over to the two men. Matt frowned a warning, but she chose to ignore it, addressing the man instead.

'You need to stay healthy for your daughter's sake. You don't want her to wake up and find you sick. She'd blame herself, and she needs to focus all her energy on getting better.' She didn't mention that his daughter was also one of the sickest in the village. No sense alarming him more than he already was.

The man didn't glance in her direction, not even once. 'Who is this woman you've brought with you? A new wife?'

Matt rubbed a hand over the back of his neck and twisted his head slightly to the right as if physically trying to relieve the pain. 'She's a doctor with *Projeto Vida.*'

'Your wife was also a doctor.'

'My wife was a nurse.'

Stevie hadn't known that. Matt had been very tense over the last week and a half, and it seemed to have more to do with her than with the dengue outbreak. She'd assumed it was because of their living conditions. But now she wondered if it was more than that. Surely he didn't have a problem with female doctors in general? She knew some cultures had a difficult time accepting women in a primary role, but hopefully Matt hadn't picked up that attitude while working here.

'She's not Brazilian,' the man continued, stating the obvious.

'No. She's American, like I am.'

'Her Portuguese is different than yours.' For the first time, the man looked at her, and she saw both intelligence and distrust in his dark eyes. Her heart sank. The last thing she wanted to do was make waves. Would the man try to keep her from helping his daughter?

'She hasn't been in Brazil as long as I have. She's a very good doctor.' Matt deftly sidestepped the question.

'You should pay her bride price and make her stay with you, then,' the man said. 'She will soon learn our ways.'

Stevie's brows went up. 'Bride price?'

Matt must have seen the shock on her face because he took her hand and gave it a warning squeeze. 'Bride prices are uncommon in my culture, so I gladly married her without one.'

Her heart flipped in her chest. He'd warned her they might have to pretend to be husband and wife, but the last village had been so accepting of her presence, she'd hoped Matt was mistaken. The warm flush of pleasure that rushed up her spine at his words had also surprised her.

He'd *gladly* married her.

'She must be worth much to you, then.' The man glanced over at the shrouded pallet a short distance away. 'My daughter is also worth much, in the eyes of her father. The village will pay any price, if you can save her.'

Matt frowned. 'We'll do our best. You don't need to pay us anything.'

'I need to go back over there to check on her,' Stevie said in English.

A few minutes later he squatted by her side beneath the mosquito netting. 'He used the repellent, thanks to you.'

'So did you both agree on his daughter's monetary value and which currency should be used?'

'I know it's hard to understand his line of reasoning, but suffice it to say this village isn't as progressive as some of the others.' Matt took hold of her chin and coaxed her to look at him. His fingers were dry and deliciously cool against her overheated skin. 'He's the village chief, Stevie. You took a big risk speaking to him without permission.'

His words stung and reminded her of the reason she was in Brazil in the first place.

Dr. Wilson doesn't follow hospital protocol.

But there hadn't been time. Her tiny patient had been fighting for his life, and his parents had been desperate. As desperate as the chief was to save his own daughter. Unfortunately, in the Western world there were rules to follow and miles of red tape to wade through for most medical procedures. There were lawsuits and malpractice insurance to consider. The tests she'd run had said the infant didn't have time for Stevie to make her case. So she'd bypassed the system in the same way she'd bypassed the baby's heart, giving him the surgery he needed. The saving of a life should have mattered—it should have meant something to those in charge. In the end, her ex had twisted things, making sure the only thing in evidence was her flouting of authority.

She shook her head to clear it. 'I'm sorry. I didn't know he was the chief.'

'I should have made it clearer. We can continue coming here only as long as the chief allows it, so I need you to keep a low profile until the worst of the crisis is over. There are rumblings that the medicine man wants us out of here.'

That surprised her. 'Even though it means people might die?'

'His hold over them weakens if people lose faith in him. I've been coming to this particular village for the last six years, and there's never been a problem until—'

'Until I showed up.'

'That's not what I was going to say.' He let go of her chin and brushed back a strand of hair the breeze had blown across her face. 'I'm not sure what will happen if the chief's daughter dies.'

'She won't. We won't let her.'

A shadow darkened his eyes. 'It's not always up to us.'

Stevie bit her lip. 'No, you're right. All we can do is our best.'

'And when that's not enough?'

'Then we pray.' The words were out before she could stop them.

Rather than scoff at her naivety, he murmured, 'Start praying, then.'

Matt's fingers, which had started out tucking her hair behind her ear, now lingered on her cheek, his thumb strumming across it with slow gentle strokes. He hadn't touched her since they'd arrived at the village four days ago, so the sensation was shocking…intoxicating. Her resolve to keep her distance crumbled, and she couldn't stop herself from leaning into his hand.

His glance fell to her mouth, and the breath whooshed from her lungs.

Lordy, was he going to kiss her?

The woman on the pallet stirred and cried out in her sleep, breaking whatever spell had fallen over them.

Matt stood so fast, a draft of air swept over her. 'I need to check on the other patients.'

Before she could say or do anything, he was gone. She stared down at her shaking hands as if they belonged to someone else. Taking a deep breath, she tried to help the chief's sick daughter find a more comfortable position, all the while convincing herself that Matt's touch hadn't affected her. It had to be nerves… and exhaustion. A good night's sleep, and she'd be as good as new.

Sure she would. As precious a commodity as sleep was these days, she had a feeling it wouldn't change a thing.

Her throat contracted, making it difficult to breathe. And she had no idea where to find an alternate solution, because she hadn't even begun to understand the problem.

Why had he stroked her cheek?

He'd known from the second she'd massaged his neck that touching her again would be a bad idea. Her soft, fragrant form had done awful things to his equilibrium as she'd stood behind him, her silky hair sliding over his shoulder from time to time as she'd worked. Not since his wife had died had he been hit with a lust so strong that it had kicked his feet from under him.

And that's *all* it was. Lust.

He sat on a log facing the river, a pile of mosquito nets to his left. Taking his time, he checked each one for holes or defects, having to repeatedly force his mind back to the task. The jungle around him hummed with activity, and a couple of tribesmen knelt in hand-crafted canoes, tossing fishing nets into the water.

People had to eat, even during an epidemic. Some of these men had ill family members, but they had to keep going—keep working.

Which was what Matt should be doing. But he'd needed to get away for a little while. Everywhere he went, Stevie was there, her long fingers deftly swabbing brows, her melodic voice murmuring to those in distress.

Her every action seemed to ignite his senses and send them spinning out of control.

She'd come to Brazil to help people—just like he had. Maybe that was part of what drew him to her. He'd known in medical school this was what he wanted to do. He'd married Vickie soon after finishing his internship and had talked her into giving it a try. They'd ended up staying.

And because of that decision, his wife was gone. If they'd stayed in a nice safe hospital inside the United States, she'd probably still be alive…their child would be growing. Thriving.

He balled his hand into a fist, the netting bunching around it, and tried not to think about the baby that had died inside his wife's womb. He stared across the water at the lush jungle on the other side of the river, wanting to push the memories away, but they came at him in waves. She'd only been four months along when she'd contracted dengue. And when she'd fallen ill, she'd been more worried about the baby than herself.

Seeing the chief's daughter writhing on that bed, her belly swollen with child, had brought it all back. And having Stevie fret over the baby's well-being…

He couldn't touch her again.

'Matt!' His name coming from somewhere behind him

brought him back to the present. He twisted on the log and saw Stevie hurrying toward him from across the clearing.

'What's wrong?'

'I've been trying to find you for the last half-hour.' She reached him, her breath coming in quick gusts. 'Nilson sent me.'

'And?' He avoided looking at her, busying himself with untangling the mosquito net that was still clenched between his fingers.

She knelt in front of him, stopping his hands with her own. 'The tribal healer is demanding to meet with you. Right now.'

CHAPTER NINE

'IF THE chief's daughter lives, there will be a celebration in your honor. If she dies...'

The medicine man's voice had trailed off, but Matt could read between the lines. *Projeto Vida* had official NGO status in Brazil, but if Matt and Stevie suddenly disappeared, no one would come looking for them, except maybe Tracy. Matt's one remaining brother hadn't seen him in so long it might be years before he realized Matt had gone missing.

They'd been given until sundown to make their decision. Either they stayed and fought for Belini's life or they were to leave and never come back. And in reality, while the chief was the symbolic head of the village, it was the medicine man who wielded the real power, and he flexed that muscle every chance he got.

Going against him wasn't an option.

The minutes ticked by, the only sound the low hum of *Projeto Vida's* generator as it powered the boat's refrigerator and other electrical components. Stevie stood off to the side, lobbing pebbles into the water. She'd been furious with him for even considering leaving. And if it were just his life hanging in the balance he wouldn't have hesitated, but it wasn't. He'd brought Stevie here, could he face risking both their lives on a situation whose outcome was far from certain?

Stevie headed toward him, her hips weaving a delicate rhythm against the ruby backdrop of the setting sun. Her eyes glittered up at him. 'I'm not leaving. You can do whatever you want, but I won't leave that woman to die.'

'It's not your decision to make.'

'Maybe not, but I'm making it anyway. You can't force me to go.'

Anger washed over him. 'I can and I will.'

Her gaze didn't flinch. 'Then I'll find a way to come back on my own. I'll…I'll hire someone to bring me back down the river.'

And probably get herself killed in the process. Or worse. She had no idea the kinds of men who worked this river. A few were honest. But some hired themselves out as guides and then robbed their unsuspecting clients, abandoning them to their fate along the banks of the Amazon.

'Damn it, woman. You're acting like a fool.'

'Then help me save Belini.' She twisted her hair into a rope and tossed it over her left shoulder. 'If I weren't here, you'd stay. You know you would.'

But she was here.

Hell, what was he going to do? He already had the guilt of one woman's death on his conscience. Did he really want to make it two?

And if he forced her to go back? He didn't for a second believe she'd stay in Coari. She'd do exactly as she threatened. Come back and try to finish the job.

What exactly was his choice, then?

'If we treat her, we do it on my terms. You follow my lead and trust me to know how the medicine man's mind works.'

Her eyes widened, and she took a step closer, until she stood a mere foot away. 'Does this mean we're staying?'

He had to force himself not to retreat. 'On two conditions. The first is that you listen to me. The second is that if things start to go south, and I decide we need to leave, you come with me, no questions asked.'

'Oh, Matt, thank you. You won't regret it.'

He already did, because she was now so close that her light feminine scent rose on the heated air to swirl around him in dizzying eddies. Her lips, soft and inviting, lay far too close for comfort.

Moist. Kissable. Doing crazy things to his head.

If she asked him to walk through hot coals, he'd agree. Without hesitation.

She laid a hand on his arm. 'I only wish I could—'

Before she had a chance to finish her sentence, the medicine man appeared with two other men from the village. Matt's hands unclenched, and he took a step back, a less pleasant kind of tension rising within him.

'You have decided to stay?'

Matt nodded. 'We have.'

'Then you both will stay at the village—separately—with two host families, as we agreed. Not on your boat.'

Stevie's eyes went wide before looking wildly in his direction. The fear he saw in their depths did him in.

He stepped in front of her. No way would he let anyone drag Stevie away from him. 'I didn't agree to separate quarters. We are married. We prefer to stay together.'

'It will be easier for you to honor our agreement if you don't have access to the woman.'

So much for his idea of them sneaking out of the village in secret if things didn't go the way he'd hoped. The medicine man must have realized this as well. 'I need her help with the patients.'

The shaman folded his arms over his chest. 'You shall have it. But you'll tend them separately. No contact until things with the chief's daughter are settled.'

Not good.

'Then I refuse to—'

Stevie gripped his hand. 'I'll be okay,' she said in English. 'I can do this.'

Her voice trembled, and he got the impression she was trying to convince herself more than him.

Dammit. He couldn't believe he'd dragged her into this mess. He'd been traveling among these villages for many years, but Stevie was a city girl. She had no experience dealing with tribal mentality. Of course she'd be terrified. He would too if he were in her shoes.

His fingers tightened around hers. 'I think we should stay together.'

'But his terms—'

'Yeah, well, I'm having second thoughts about agreeing to them.'

She gave him a shaky smile. 'Hopefully, they're taking your reluctance to let me go as a sign of affection. Very husband-like. Good job.'

It was anything but a job. And the thought of not seeing her for days, possibly longer, hit him harder than it should have.

'If you run into trouble, come to the boat. I'll tell Tiago and Nilson to be on the lookout for you. They'll come and find me.'

'I'll be fine. Don't worry. Let's just tend our patients and get through this.'

He couldn't resist touching the twist of sleek hair that still hung over her shoulder. 'You've worked hard today. Rest. I'll see to the patients tonight.'

'Are you sure?'

The annoyed rustling from the medicine man reminded him they were waiting to lead Stevie away to God knew where.

'I am,' he said. 'I'll try to talk some sense into the chief while I'm at it.'

She nodded, glancing toward the three men who'd moved a couple of steps forward. Matt forced his hand away from her hair and back to his side.

'I think they want me to go with them,' she said. 'I'll see you tomorr—soon, I hope.'

Soon.

As soon as they knew whether Belini was going to live…

Or die.

CHAPTER TEN

'Mmm, delicious! What's this called?' Stevie sat cross-legged on the ground and took another bite of the bread-like substance her hostess had prepared for breakfast.

'It's called *bejú.*'

She cocked her head, her eyes unconsciously scanning the still dark area hoping to catch a glimpse of her new 'husband'.

Husband.

Ha! Nothing like jumping from a fiancé you thought you knew but realized you didn't to a husband you literally didn't know at all.

Good going, Stevie, girl.

Returning her attention to the shy young woman who sprinkled what looked like dry white powder over a hot skillet, Stevie watched in amazement as the particles magically coalesced into a solid whole. '*Beijo*? You mean, like a kiss?'

The woman giggled, her brown eyes dancing as, with an expert flick of her wrist, she flipped the tortilla to the other side. 'No, not a kiss. *Bejúuuu.*' She drew out the last syllable, emphasizing it.

Tipping the skillet to slide the bread onto a plate, she then slathered it with butter and folded it in half. She offered the fresh hot bread to Stevie, who'd just polished off her other piece.

'You eat this one,' Stevie protested.

The woman ignored her request and pushed the bread onto Stevie's wooden plate.

Unable to resist, she picked it up and took a bite, groaning in ecstasy. 'I sure hope these aren't as fattening as pancakes.'

'Pan-cakes?'

Stevie laughed. 'I'll show you someday.' Her laughter caught in her throat as a dark familiar shape strolled from the direction of the river, heading toward the chief's daughter's sickbed. The morning sun was just peeking over the horizon and backlit the man's form, but she knew without a doubt it was Matt. His hands were stuffed in his pockets, a habit that seemed ingrained. What wasn't normal, however, was the slight stoop of his broad shoulders.

She started to wave to him, but remembered the medicine man's words and stopped herself. She didn't want to risk endangering their precarious situation, especially when the chief's daughter was reaching the critical stage of the illness. Instead, she turned her attention back to her hostess and tried to concentrate on what the woman was saying.

Their patients had been cleverly divvied up by the chief so there was no overlap, and no chance to talk to each other.

No longer hungry, she nevertheless forced down the last few bites, managing a smile that felt a bit more watery than usual.

She would not dwell on the fact that she should be back in New York, blissfully planning her wedding, the horror of finding her fiancé in bed with a colleague banished to the land of bad dreams.

As was the disciplinary note in her file.

At least the baby she'd operated on was safe in his mother's arms. That's all that mattered in the end. The board of directors could fire her. Roast her. Tear up her medical license. But nothing could take away the joy that poured into her when the baby had given his first strong cry as he'd come out from under the anesthesia. Or the excitement of seeing those once-blue lips flush a deep pink as his repaired heart pumped life-giving blood to the farthest reaches of his tiny body. She sighed. That moment had been worth it all.

She wanted to feel that same joy as she watched the chief's daughter recover. But there was no chance of that, as they'd assigned Stevie to the least ill of the villagers, giving Matt all the tough cases, including Belini's. He must be totally exhausted by now.

'Can I help wash the dishes before I start my rounds?' she said.

The woman shooed her away from the cooking area before she could touch a single dirty plate.

Deciding to go down to the river and dip her dusty feet before heading off to work, she wandered down to the water's edge. Her wet flip-flops would just attract more grime, but the water would at least cool her senses.

What was wrong with her? Surely seeing Matt for a few seconds shouldn't affect her like this?

She waded into the river, until it just barely covered her feet, leaving her shoes on in case of sharp stones. Closing her eyes, she sighed as the silken flow caressed her skin.

'Not worried about anacondas?'

The low voice came out of nowhere, and a shriek climbed the walls of her throat. A firm hand clapped over her mouth just in time, preventing the sound from exiting. 'Shh, we're not supposed to be together, remember?'

Matt. She'd recognize that low murmur anywhere. And as soon as he let her go, she was going to kill him for scaring her like that.

She swallowed. Except that the sensation of his bare feet against hers and the pressure of his thighs against her backside shoved the murderous thoughts aside, replacing them with something else altogether.

He edged her out of the water, hand still over her mouth, and then half carried her to the stand of trees growing along the bank. Once hidden within the thick growth, he released her.

Stevie whirled to face him, a sudden sense of panic welling in her chest as she realized something might be wrong. 'Is Belini okay?'

'She's fine for the moment. Keep your voice down,' he warned, glancing back toward the river.

'What are you doing here, then? The last time I saw you, you were headed in the opposite direction.'

'Trying to avoid me?'

At least it wasn't *her* who was flouting protocol this time. 'I'm trying to play by the rules.'

'So I see.' His gaze ran over her face before lingering on her throat for a minute. A frown appeared between his brows. Lifting his hand, he picked up her mother's gold band, which was normally tucked safely beneath her T-shirts. But her blouse today had a deep V neckline that exposed the ring's hiding place. He looked up. 'Is this what I think it is?'

'Yes, but it's not mine.' The words came out faster than she'd have liked, but she had no desire to relive the pain and humiliation of catching her fiancé with another woman. Of knowing that for whatever reason she hadn't been enough for him. Neither did she want to remember the devastating cost of his betrayal in both personal and professional terms. Maybe someday she'd be able to share those things with someone. But not now. Not when the emotions were still so raw and fresh.

She met his eyes. 'The ring was my mother's. She passed away two years ago. It seems silly, but it helps me keep her close.'

He toyed with the delicate chain that held the ring next to her heart. The sensation of his fingers sliding across her skin sent a ripple of need down her spine. She gritted her teeth and prayed he didn't notice her strange reaction.

'I'm sorry,' he said. 'It's none of my business. I shouldn't have asked.'

'It's okay.'

His glance left hers, going back to the ring. 'I don't know that much about you, other than what was on your job application. And some of that was suspect, thanks to Tracy.' The slight smile disappeared. 'With everything that's happened over the last several days… Well, the ring made me wonder if you had someone special waiting for you back home.'

'There's no one. Not any more.' She was shocked to realize her feelings for Michael had dried up as surely as a drop of water in the desert. When had that happened?

'But there was.' Something dark passed across his face.

'Yes. But it's over.'

The acknowledgement was easier than she'd expected. And maybe it was due to the fact that she knew less about the man in front of her than he apparently knew about her. She hadn't even had a short bio to go by, like he'd had. In fact, she only knew about his wife's death because she'd discovered the handwriting in his medical reference. But Matt himself had shared nothing about his life outside the ship. Not even in passing.

He was right. They knew nothing about each other. She suddenly wanted to change that.

'My mother committed suicide.' The words were out before she could hold them back.

A few seconds passed, and she wondered if he'd even heard her. Then his hand fisted around the ring, pulling the chain taut against the back of her neck and bringing her a step closer to him. 'Ah, hell, Stevie. I'm sorry.'

Stevie licked her lips, trying to keep her words steady. 'She was in a lot of emotional pain. No one realized how much...' she pulled in a deep breath '...until it was too late.'

'Your father?'

The man she'd worshipped as a child had turned out to be a bastard who'd driven her mother to the depths of despair. And possibly the reason Michael's final betrayal had marked her so deeply. 'My father...cheated. He's no longer a part of my life.'

'I'm sorry.' His eyes searched hers. 'What about the rest of your family? Do they know you're here with me?'

With me.

The intimacy of the words made her heart flip, until she realized he was simply asking if they knew she was in Brazil. Not specifically with him.

'My friends do.' And how pitiful did that sound? The girl with no family. With no one to care about her.

He let go of her necklace and traced a finger along her collarbone. 'You should wear long sleeves and a higher neckline.'

The breath she'd sucked in wheezed back out in a rush of sound. She was suddenly aware of their isolation—of the cool press of trees that screened their presence from casual passers-by. They could do anything back here, and no one would know. She swallowed. 'I—I used repellent.'

His mouth quirked. 'Too bad it doesn't work on bigger pests.'

She couldn't help herself and smiled back.

His eyes dropped to her lips and held, then he took a sudden step back, his hands returning to his sides. 'I checked on Belini this morning. She's better. We can tell the chief we think she'll fully recover. Then we can leave.'

'You think?' Stevie frowned. 'But she's pregnant. Are you willing to take that chance?'

'Yes.'

She didn't believe him. 'No, you're not. And even if you were, I'm not. Besides, you don't know that others won't be infected by the ones who are sick. The incubation period hasn't passed yet.'

His throat moved, his Adam's apple taking a quick dive. 'And you could get it, if we stick around too long. On the boat I can at least offer you some prot—' His voice trailed off.

'Protection?' Her chest contracted at the stark despair she heard in his voice. So that's what this was about. She moved forward, touching his arm. 'You're not God, Matt. You can't protect the whole world.'

Something unbearably sad passed through his eyes. 'It's a good thing, because the world would be in trouble if I were.'

'I don't believe that. You're doing a good thing here.' She forced a smile and put her hand to his cheek. 'Speaking of which, I should go and see to my own patients.'

'I've already checked on them.' His hand came up to cover hers, his palm warm against her skin.

'On all of them? But you were told to stay away from my assigned cases. The medicine man made a rule, remember?'

'I was also told to stay away from you, and yet here I am.' He gave a slow smile. 'I don't *always* follow the rules.'

'You don't?'

His gaze dropped again to her lips. 'Not all of them.'

The touch of his fingers sliding across her cheek and burrowing into her hair made her knees turn to water. 'Are you about to break one right now?' she whispered.

'Oh, yeah.' His head lowered until he was just a heartbeat away. 'Can you guess which one?'

CHAPTER ELEVEN

RULES. Who needed rules?

The second he touched his mouth to Stevie's he was lost. He'd fantasized about this kiss from the moment he'd seen her sitting on that suitcase looking so forlorn at the airport. Oh, he'd denied it, acting like some macho hulk who could take anything life dished out, but he couldn't pretend. Not any more.

He was proving that. Right here. Right now.

And when her fingers climbed his chest and clutched at his shoulders, he growled low in his throat. He'd been content to go about his work and leave thoughts about family and future in the past, figuring it was the sacrifice he had to make to help others.

But if Stevie had the same goals as he did...

He angled his mouth to deepen the kiss, even as other, more troubling thoughts began surfacing. It didn't matter what her goals were. He'd left certain things out of his life for a reason. He didn't want to be responsible for anyone other than himself and his patients. Emotional attachments meant he couldn't do his job properly, and when he allowed his feelings to interfere, people got hurt.

People died.

His heart sank. What he was doing was wrong on so many different levels.

The touch of Stevie's tongue against his jarred him fully back to reality. His fingers slid from her hair and went to her shoulders, using light pressure to break contact with her mouth.

She blinked up at him. 'W-what's wrong?'

His teeth clenched, once, twice, three times before he won the war over his body and relocated his voice. 'I'm sorry.' The hoarse quality of the words made him cringe.

'Sorry?'

'I shouldn't have done that.'

Hurt flashed through her eyes, and she took a step back, shoving a lock of hair out of her face. 'I see.'

She did? Because he had no idea what the hell was going on here. 'I guess I'm not a rule-breaker after all.'

Her lips tightened. 'Right. Well, maybe you've just never run across a situation that made those so-called rules seem unimportant.'

That's where she was wrong. He'd found it. But that didn't mean he had to follow his impulses and greedily satisfy his own wants. Because that's all it would be. That's all it could be. A few snatched hours of heaven in her arms. He wasn't willing to risk more than that. Not for anyone.

'Most rules are put in place for a reason.'

'Like the save-the-chief's-daughter-or-you'll-be-sorry rule given by the medicine man? I can really see the validity behind that one.' She snatched her hair into a ponytail and tossed it over her left shoulder.

'Like I said, she's getting better, so it's a moot point. We should still think about leaving.'

'There could be others who'll become ill. You have no way of knowing which ones will develop dengue shock syndrome or the hemorrhagic version, do you?' There was a big pause. 'Neither you nor your wife knew she'd become one of those statistics.'

As soon as the words were out of her mouth, she blanched, turning a pasty shade of white. 'Oh, Matt, I shouldn't have said that. It's just that she seemed to think she'd be up and around in a week or two, right?'

He swallowed, remembering his discovery of the heart-wrenching account of her illness. 'We both thought the worst was behind her. Until she got the first nose bleed.'

She touched his arm. 'Exactly. That's why we have to stay. What if the same thing happens to Belini, and we're not here to help?' She paused. 'How will you live with yourself knowing we might have done something to prevent it?'

He filled in the blanks: *the way he could have—should have—prevented his wife's death.*

His shoulders slumped. 'You're willing to see this through to the end?'

'Yes.'

'And if—'

The sound of his name being shouted up at the village interrupted what he'd been about to say.

Tiago. He'd never heard the man raise his voice. Ever.

'Something's wrong. I have to go.' He turned to leave, only to have her grab his arm.

'I'm coming with you, rules or no rules.'

He nodded, his heart racing as a hefty dose of adrenaline hit his system.

By the time they reached the village, a cluster of people had gathered outside Belini's hut.

On the periphery, Tiago waited, his eyes obviously searching for them. Matt strode over to him. 'What's going on?'

His crew member shook his head. 'I'm not sure. The medicine man's just gone inside.'

'Why?' The shaman had seemed okay with leaving Belini's care to them a day earlier.

'I think she's gotten worse. Her husband tried to find you a few minutes ago, and when he couldn't, he came back with the medicine man and the chief.'

A wave of guilt crashed over him. While he'd been dragging Stevie into the bushes—making out with her—all hell had broken loose. Belini had been his responsibility. No one else's.

'Matt said she was fine a half-hour ago,' Stevie said, as if to defend him.

When a sudden scream pierced the air around them. He didn't wait for permission, he went through the door flap of the mud dwelling, Stevie right on his heels.

What he found made his skin crawl. Belini was curled in a

fetal position, moaning, a small pool of blood on the mat beneath her. Her husband stood to one side, his hands clenched.

Could she have gone hemorrhagic despite how she'd appeared earlier?

'Let me examine her.'

The chief, who was next to the bed, moved aside, but the medicine man eyed him and stayed where he was, spreading a pack of herbs on the ground next to the girl while chanting in the native tongue. Matt let him do his work, while quickly squatting beside Belini. He tried to reassure her as he lifted her lids to examine her eyes, then glanced at the rest of her pale face. No blood coming from her nose or ears.

'Matt, I think she's going into labor.' Stevie's voice came from just over his left shoulder, speaking in English.

Not good. The girl wasn't due for several more weeks.

The stress of the fever could have triggered premature labor. His teeth ground together in frustration. And for her to try to deliver a baby in such a weakened state could prove disastrous.

Coaxing her from her side onto her back, he felt the truth the second his hand settled on her belly. His own gut tightened.

Stevie was right.

He could pray the rock-hard stomach was evidence of harmless Braxton-Hicks contractions rather than the beginning of actual labor, but, judging from the beads of sweat on the girl's upper lip, that prayer would probably be in vain. Still speaking in low English so as not to alarm anyone, he glanced at Stevie, who was kneeling next to him. 'I need my bag. It's by the main campfire.'

She nodded and hurried out of the hut without a word.

Matt went over to the chief. 'Can you ask everyone to leave the room?' He hesitated. 'Everyone…except the medicine man?'

Now was not the time to fight over who was in charge. Besides, he needed all the help he could get, and if the man's rituals could reach someone in the spirit world, he wasn't about to interfere.

'What is wrong with her?' The chief's voice was strong and sure, but Matt got the feeling it was for the benefit of the others in the hut. Underneath that fierce façade beat the heart of a father—one who was mentally tearing his hair out with each terrible moan his daughter made.

'I'm not sure yet. But it's possible she's going to have her baby.'

The chief stood straighter. 'Then I will call for one of the midwives to take your place. A man should not be here.'

Matt thought fast, remembering Stevie's comments about rules sometimes needing to be broken. 'Stevie will be here, but she might need my help.' He glanced at the medicine man, knowing he was taking in every word, even if he seemed lost in his own preparations. 'I lost my wife to dengue, remember? I won't let your daughter follow that path. Not if it's in my power to save her.'

The chief gave a visible swallow before nodding. 'Yes. I believe you.' He laid a hand on Belini's husband's shoulder. 'Do you wish this man to treat your wife?'

Belini's husband glanced down at her writhing form, then his anguished eyes met Matt's. A wealth of meaning passed between the two men. He nodded at the chief and glanced at the others in the room. 'Yes, I wish it. Do as he says.'

As Matt ushered them out of the hut, Stevie arrived with his bag. He knew he had to walk a fine line here. The medicine man, just as he'd expected, hadn't left with the others—he meant to watch their every move.

'You're going to take the lead,' he said to her, making sure to keep the conversation in Portuguese to prove his transparency. 'The chief is only letting me stay because I've had experience with dengue. Men aren't welcome at birthing ceremonies.'

Stevie's eyes widened. 'What? Surely the tribal elders can make an exception in this case.'

Losing his wife had been almost too terrible to bear, and he wouldn't wish that on Belini's husband or anyone else. But her death was allowing him access, where he'd normally have none. He meant to make the most of the opportunity.

'I told them you might need my help.' His glance went to the medicine man, hoping Stevie would follow his train of thought and not argue the point.

Thankfully, she nodded her understanding. 'How likely is she to hemorrhage during the birth?'

'She's spotting, but she's not bleeding anywhere else that I can see. Let's just take it one step at a time.'

As he prepared the instruments, Stevie moved in close to the woman's head and placed her palm gently on the girl's cheek to capture her attention. 'Hi, sweetheart. I know you're scared and that you don't feel well, but I think your baby wants to meet you.'

'Tired.' Belini groaned as another contraction hit. 'Hurts so badly.'

'I know, honey. But we're here. We're going to help you.' She didn't wait for the woman's answer, knowing she'd already turned inward to deal with the contraction. As soon as it let up, she held Belini's hands, giving them a quick squeeze. 'When you feel the pressure building again, I want you to take a deep breath and release it.'

Two hours of pushing and still no birth.

Stevie used the flats of her hands on the next contraction, hoping the steady downward pressure would coax the baby further into the birth canal. Speaking with low, calming murmurs, her own heart raced with fear as she watched Matt work.

With each push, the baby inched closer, only to be drawn back to its original position when the contraction was over. Exhaustion was taking hold. Soon there would be no choice but to take her aboard the boat and attempt an emergency Cesarean. But she knew Matt was afraid the anesthesia would be too much for the woman at this point—even if the chief allowed it.

He swore softly. 'The baby's still sunny side up. There's no way he'll fit like this—the pelvis is too narrow. I'm going to have to try turning its head again on the next contraction.'

Stevie cringed, knowing the agony Belini had experienced during the previous two attempts, but she forced herself to collect a deep breath and nod her understanding. Matt knew what he was doing. Still, the other two tries had ended with the baby stubbornly reverting to its original position, with the back of his head firmly pressing on his mother's spine. A much harder way to deliver. And for someone of Belini's petite size and debilitated condition…almost impossible.

'Here we go. Help her push.'

Stevie bore down, noting the stiff concentration on Matt's face, the muscle in his jaw contracting as he felt for the baby's head and attempted to rotate it manually. Belini's weak moans tore at her heart.

'Come on, sweetie,' she whispered to the baby. 'Stay where Uncle Matt puts you.'

'Tell her to keep pushing. If we can move him down the canal a little bit more, his body should turn in unison with the head.' There was a pause. 'Almost there. Keep going.'

'*Empurre.*' The soft command was as much for Stevie's benefit as it was for Belini's. She kept her hands firm on the girl's abdomen, her fingers sensing each and every inch of ground they gained.

'Wait! Wait! Don't push!' Matt's harsh shout stopped everyone in their tracks. Even the medicine man stopped his incessant chanting.

'What is it?' She held back the fear that gnawed at her throat.

'Head's out.' He looked up and although his hair was plastered to his head and sweat had worn tracks down his face, his shaky smile lit up the darkening room. 'The hard part's over. Now we just need to ease the shoulders out.'

Stevie's heart stopped then started beating again. She leaned close to Belini's ear. 'Your baby's about to be born.'

Within ten minutes an angry-sounding cry split the room, strong and sure, as if the baby—and not his mother—had won this particular round.

Belini's exhausted brown eyes met her own. 'He cries.'

A laugh came out unbidden. 'Yes, he does.'

'And a "he" it is. The baby's a boy,' said Matt, working to clear the baby's nose and throat. 'Small, but healthy and pink.'

'Thank God.' Stevie's knees went rubbery, and she dropped back onto her haunches. 'Any signs of dengue?'

Matt wrapped the baby in a clean blanket. 'Not a trace, but then again, it's…' There was a pause and Stevie could swear his voice caught for a second. When he continued, the sensation was gone. 'It's rare for the fetus to be affected.'

She looked at him, trying to gauge the change in his mood. He should be elated. He *had* been a couple of minutes ago. But now he seemed flat, as if all emotion had been sucked out of him.

He's exhausted.

That had to be it. She felt like a wet noodle herself.

Without a word, the medicine man folded up the small cloth that held his amulets and incense herbs and tucked it into a pouch that hung around his neck. He stood and went through the flap on the hut.

Matt put the baby into Belini's arms. The woman glanced at him as her fingers stroked one of the infant's hands. 'He's so tiny. I fear I will break him.'

When Matt didn't respond, Stevie scooted closer and smoothed damp strands of hair from the woman's forehead. 'You won't. He's tough. As tough as his mama.'

Belini nodded, lost in that special world in which only she and her baby existed.

Matt climbed to his feet, hands clenched by his side, and Stevie's heart ached at how alone he appeared. He'd worked so hard, she expected him to express relief that it was over, or to break into another of those rare smiles like the one he'd given her when the baby's head had crowned.

'Are you okay?' she asked, standing up and laying her hand on his arm.

His skin seemed icy, despite the heat inside the hut.

Something was definitely wrong.

His eyes shut for a moment, then he turned away to gather his equipment. 'I'm fine. Just tired.'

So was she. So was Belini.

This was different.

'Matt—'

'Just leave it alone, Stevie.' He turned to face her. 'Belini's fine. The baby's fine. *Everything's* fine.'

She blinked. Not everything. But like he said, now was not the time to push it. 'I'm glad it all worked out.'

'Yeah. Me, too.'

Before she knew what was happening, he'd shoved through the doorway, and the chief came in, along with Belini's husband. All of them started speaking at once. The chief's face was the softest she'd seen it since their arrival. He stared down at the pair reclining on the pallet.

'They are both well?' he asked.

She nodded, giving him a reassuring smile. 'Belini needs a lot of rest, she's still ill from the dengue, but the baby is healthy.'

'A boy?' Belini's husband glanced up at her.

'Yes.' She gritted her teeth, expecting the normal macho swagger to appear. Instead she was surprised when the young man knelt and brushed his fingers across Belini's cheek. 'A girl would have looked like you.'

Belini smiled, and the young couple's eyes caught and held. A prick of tears appeared behind Stevie's lids.

Okay, so her own reactions were a bit off kilter, too, so who was she to judge Matt's response? Adrenaline affected everyone differently.

'I'll leave you alone for a while,' she said. 'But make sure you let Belini rest, okay?'

The chief nodded. 'I'll send for some of the women to help with the baby.'

'Good idea.' She ducked out of the tent, intending to search for Matt, but she spotted him as soon as she emerged. He stood about fifty yards away with the medicine man. The two either didn't see her or they ignored her. Judging from the harsh set of Matt's cheeks, she guessed they were arguing.

As soon as she started toward them, though, Matt's eyes met hers. He gave his head a slight shake, telling her to stay put.

So he had seen her. She stood there and brushed the dust from her shirt, undecided whether she should ignore his unspoken warning and demand to know what was going on or simply go to the boat and shower. If she made the shaman angry, it could harm what Matt was trying to accomplish.

A shower it was, then.

Thankfully she found Tiago by the shore. 'How is she?' he asked.

She forced a smile to her face. 'She and the baby are fine.'

'That is good.' He nodded his head. 'Very good.'

'Could you row me to the boat?'

'Of course.' He glanced past her. 'Is Mateus not with you?'

'No. He's…tired.' Those had been his words, right?

And if he'd lied, tough. He could find his own way back to the medical ship. Or maybe he wouldn't bother, he'd just go to his host's hut and not bother to say goodnight.

She stepped into the dinghy and flopped down onto the nearest bench. Tiago took up the oars and started rowing, while Stevie stared morosely into the murky water of the Rio Preto.

Matt's mood was obviously catching. She gave a soft snort of disgust and muttered under her breath, 'Like the man said: Belini's fine. The baby's fine. *Everything's* fine.'

CHAPTER TWELVE

'THEY want to give us a wedding ceremony? Why?' Stevie's eyes flashed at him. 'They think we're already married.'

'Remember the celebration the medicine man promised to throw in our honor if Belini recovered? And how the chief was concerned about the lack of a bride price? Well, this is the village's way of thanking us.'

He didn't need this. Not today. Delivering that baby had taken what little was left of his soul and wrung it dry. All he could see was Vickie fighting for every breath, the fear etched across her face. Not for herself, but for the baby. If she died, their baby died, she'd whispered.

Don't let our baby die.

But he had. He'd let both of them die. And Stevie had almost witnessed the wave of grief that had crashed over him as he'd looked down at the new mother and her baby.

Alive.

Even now. God help him…even now, something inside him threatened to break loose.

'Matt?' Her voice brought him back to the question at hand.

He cleared his throat. 'I assumed the medicine man meant us to be honored guests at a normal tribal celebration. But he's insisting on doing it this way, and so is the chief. Especially now. The chief doesn't want to risk his grandson's well-being.'

Her brows shot up. 'He thinks the medicine man will put a curse on the baby or something?'

'It's a possibility.'

'Surely he doesn't believe—'

'He does.' There was a pause. 'This is their life. Their culture. Would you take that risk if it were your baby?'

A furrow appeared between Stevie's eyes. 'Probably not. What are we going to do?'

'We could always leave. Right now. They wouldn't notice for a couple of hours.'

'Would they come after us?'

'Doubtful.'

She nodded. 'Would we be allowed back in the future if we refused to participate? Or if we left without warning?'

Did he even care? At the moment, no. But later, when things returned to normal…when his emotions were no longer being dragged across a jagged set of rocks, he might. 'No, I probably wouldn't be welcomed back with open arms.'

'You mean "we".'

'Excuse me?'

'*We* wouldn't be welcomed back with open arms.'

Right. Not if he had anything to do with it. Stevie wasn't coming back here with him. Ever.

'Fine,' he lied. 'We.'

'Belini's better, but is she well enough to be left without medical care?'

He dragged a hand through his hair. The last thing he needed was to be reminded of Belini and her baby. 'Listen. I just came to relay the medicine man's wishes. You tell me what you want to do.'

'You *want* to leave, don't you? Even if it could be detrimental to Belini's health.'

'I'm not thrilled about having a tribal wedding, no. Pretending to be married was one thing, but this is something else entirely.'

Stevie sucked in a quick breath and pressed her hand to her stomach. Then her chin lifted. 'That doesn't answer my original question.'

Suddenly angry that she kept finding his weakest point and probing it again and again, he stepped closer. 'Yes. I want to leave. Right now.'

She flinched, but instead of backing away her fingers touched his hand. 'Is it because of the illness? Because of your wife?'

The wave of pain beat against the wall of his heart with such force he thought his knees would give out. The urge to grab Stevie and yank her close, to bury his face in her hair and hold her until the horror of the past receded, welled up and threatened to spill over into action. He stood there, hands clenched, waiting for the agony to cease. Waiting for his legs to steady.

Long moments passed as they stared at each other.

'Yes. It's because of my wife.' The husky words came out before he could stop them.

Stevie's hand, still touching his, curled around his fingers, gripping tight. 'It must have been hard last night, knowing—'

'She was pregnant.'

This time he knew exactly what he was saying. Stevie needed to know, in case he lost the war being waged inside him.

'Pregnant? Belini, you mean?'

'No, my wife.'

Her lips parted, eyes widening. 'Your wife was pregnant when she contracted dengue?'

He nodded.

The hand gripping his let go so suddenly, his fingers reflexively reached out to find hers again. Within a second or two, her palms settled on his shoulders.

'Oh, Matt, I had no idea. I'm so sorry.' Her eyes met his. 'And then to be faced with the very same situation last night.'

He shrugged. 'We all have to face things that make us... uncomfortable.'

'Uncomfortable. Don't you think this ranks a little higher than that?'

Yes. But that didn't mean he had to admit it. 'It was a long time ago.'

'It still hurts, though, even now.'

He took a step back dislodging her hands. 'It's over and done.'

'Is it?' Stevie's teeth came down on her lip. 'I think we need to go ahead with the celebration if that will help us see Belini's case through to the end. It might help with...things.'

His eyes narrowed. 'If you're referring to me, don't bother. I'm fine.'

'I'm serious, Matt. Let's just stay for a few more days. Take yourself out of the equation for a second. Maybe *I* need to make sure Belini completely recovers. We'll go through with the celebration.' This time she shrugged. 'It's not a legal wedding ceremony. It'll mean nothing to anyone outside this village, and certainly not to us.'

Well, that put him in his place, didn't it? 'You can't be serious.'

'Oh, but I am.' Her brows went up and she smiled. 'Let's get married.'

The bride didn't wear white.

But she did wear a shirt.

A concession for which Stevie was eternally grateful. And from the relief evident on her groom's face as his pale eyes swept over her, she wasn't the only one who was grateful that her assets remained safely under cover.

They'd placed him on a small stool in the center of a group of men. His dark hair, damp from a recent washing, lay slicked back from his forehead, and the black shirt he wore pulled tight across the taut muscles of his arms.

She swallowed—hard. Lordy, did he ever look good.

A tiny curl of smoke caught her attention and her eyes drifted down his chest until she came to a long wooden tube with a bowl at its end. He held the object tightly, his fingers curled around the stem.

A pipe of some kind.

While the giggling woman behind her urged her to move closer, Matt handed the pipe to another man, who took a couple of puffs then passed it on to the next one in line.

She stood over him, unsure what was expected of her but acutely aware of the large quantity of kohl the women had used in crafting and sculpting her eyes—she could have come straight out of a painting from ancient Egypt. Raccoons all across America would be green with envy.

A quick shiver went through her when Matt studied her, his warm fingers wrapping around hers and forcing her to bend towards him. She stooped until her ear was inches from his lips, praying the loosely draped fabric that crisscrossed key areas of her chest didn't gape and give everyone an eyeful. Not that they hadn't seen it all before, since none of the women present had anything on up top.

Matt whispered into her ear, and she closed her eyes as the silky smooth vibrations flowed across her senses and reached her innermost being. Her brain took extra care in reassembling the words until the meaning took hold. 'The pipe contains a hallucinogen. Don't breathe the smoke.'

Don't breathe the smoke.

She blinked. That couldn't be right. Then she glanced at his face and saw the truth.

He hadn't said, 'You look ravishing' or 'Are you okay?' He'd simply given the type of cold medical analysis she should have expected from him by now. A quick laugh erupted from her throat.

She straightened, noting the wide dilation of his pupils as she did. Had Mr. By-the-Book followed his own advice?

Surely the man wasn't high.

Her arched brows threw him a question, and his lips quirked in response.

'No. I didn't,' he murmured, in English. 'Although with the way you're dressed, I'm thinking maybe I should have indulged. More than once.'

Okay, maybe he hadn't told her she was beautiful, but he'd definitely noticed the large swaths of exposed skin. She smiled back, more pleased than she should have been. 'It could have been worse.'

He shifted on the stool. 'I doubt it.'

The medicine man cleared his throat behind them and waved his hand, indicating the ceremony was about to begin. Those too ill to attend had stayed in their huts, including Belini, but it looked like everyone else was anxious to witness the nuptials firsthand, including Tiago and Nilson, who stood on the periphery, grinning like loons.

Stevie resisted the impulse to roll her eyes. Surely they understood this was all a farce. If not, she'd set them straight at the first available opportunity. No need to make this trip more awkward than it already was.

Through all the dancing, feasting, and ceremonial pronouncements that followed—of which she understood nothing—she considered herself a pretty good sport. She even managed to sit next to Matt at the hand-carved banquet table and not give away how shaky she felt or how nervous his proximity made her. All in all, things had gone easier than she'd expected. The tribe hadn't even made her promise to love, honor, and obey Matt. Which was a good thing. Because she couldn't pledge to do any of it.

As the night shadows crept over the village, she breathed a sigh of relief. Until she spied a young girl carrying a banana leaf in both hands. Nestled inside lay a piece of cloth, a cork and a long, thin needle pre-threaded with a piece of dark string. A black bead knotted onto the end caught the firelight and gave an ominous wink.

Stevie swallowed. She had no idea what any of this meant, but the cork and needle gave her pause. If she wasn't mistaken…

She fingered one of her ears. They were already pierced so the worst that could happen was they would thread the bead through one of her preexisting holes. Right?

Right?

Was that needle even sterilized?

Matt's hand covered hers and squeezed. 'Relax. It's not for you.'

'Thank heavens.'

She glanced around and noted that none of the women's ears were pierced.

What was the needle for, then?

And the men…

One by one, she looked at them. Every male older than about thirteen years of age had at least one ear pierced. Maybe they were combining two ceremonies into one. She glanced around for a young initiate who might be going through a rite of passage.

The girl stopped in front of Matt with a shy smile, and the medicine man stepped forward. Stevie's lungs whooshed out a shocked breath. Surely they couldn't mean to pierce one of his ears.

'Matt,' she whispered. 'What are they doing?'

One brow cocked. 'Only *adult* men can go through the tribe's wedding rituals.'

'I don't understand.'

'Don't you?'

She blinked as awareness slowly took hold. 'That's crazy. Anyone in their right mind can tell you're a man.' As soon as the words left her mouth, hot color rushed into her face and she hurried to explain herself. 'I mean, you have chest hair and… everything.'

His lips twisted. 'Thanks. I think.'

'This is ridiculous. You're not going to let them pierce your ear.'

'Unless I'm marked as a man, I can't marry in this tribe.' He sent her a smile that made her shiver. 'You're the one who insisted on going through with this.'

'But that was before I knew they were going to punch holes in you.'

'It'll heal.'

'How can you be so blasé? What if the needle's not sterile?'

'It is. I ran it through our autoclave on the boat this morning.'

All this because of her stupid insistence on sticking around. She should have let him run while he'd had the chance.

The medicine man motioned for him to stand.

Stevie shot to her feet. 'Pierce my ear instead,' she said in loud Portuguese.

A moment's stunned silence followed her outburst, then rough laughter broke out among the male tribe members. Even the medicine man's normally expressionless eyes crinkled around the edges.

She didn't see what was so funny.

Matt turned to her. 'They think you're demanding to wear the pants of the family. That you want to be marked as the man of our union.'

If her face was red before, it had to be crimson now. 'I was just trying to help.'

He smiled. 'Trust me. You're not. But you are blushing up a storm.' His fingers slid across her steaming cheek. 'I like it.'

Turning away from her and facing the cluster of males, Matt lifted his chin. 'The role of man is mine and mine alone. I will care for my wife.'

His assertion didn't offend her; she knew the men expected it of him. What did bother her was the way her heart responded to the firm words. It softened into a pile of mush and threatened to lie down at his feet. She stopped it before it had a chance to embarrass her.

They're only words. He doesn't mean them.

Stepping forward with a cloth, the medicine man dampened it with something and then handed it to Matt. The sharp tang of rubbing alcohol stung her nose as he wiped down his own ear in preparation for the piercing.

He was doing this because of her.

She shook her head before her eyes could even think about misting over. No, he wasn't. He was doing it to continue the work here.

Don't get any ideas, Stevie. This man isn't on the market. And neither are you!

The sterilization done, Matt handed the cloth back to the medicine man, who set it aside and took up the needle and cork.

This couldn't be happening.

Matt tilted his head to the side and allowed the medicine man to slide the cork behind his earlobe. If the needle had looked wicked before, it now looked positively evil. Stevie noted there was already a black dot on Matt's ear marking the correct spot. She hadn't even noticed it before, but it had to have been placed there earlier. Before the ceremony even started.

And he said he'd already autoclaved the needle.

Which meant he'd known this was going to happen all along. He'd probably seen the ceremony countless times before. Was that why he'd tried to talk her into leaving the village with him?

Maybe she'd forced him into a situation he hadn't wanted. It wasn't like he was the type of man to voluntarily sport an earring.

The medicine man raised the needle, and Stevie couldn't stop herself. She slid her hand beneath Matt's. If he was going through with it, she was going to make sure he knew she was here. His fingers tightened around hers just as the needle speared through his ear. To Matt's credit, he didn't flinch. But she did.

When the bead was threaded through and tied off close to his ear, she soaked another cloth with more alcohol and allowed the liquid to dribble over the fresh wound. 'I'm sorry. I had no idea this was going to happen.'

He sucked in a quick breath as the sting hit. 'The work I go through just to marry you.'

She watched as the medicine man handed the implements back to the young girl who'd brought them in. He then took a palm frond and touched it to Matt's head three times. Then he met her eyes and nodded for her to bow her head. She did and the frond brushed her crown in the same way it had Matt's.

When it was done, a cheer went up. The women started dancing, and the pipe with the curling smoke began making its rounds again.

That was it.

In the tribe's eyes, they were officially married.

For better or worse.

Catching sight of Matt's freshly pierced ear just before the men dragged him away with jubilant shouts, she had a feeling things were leaning toward the latter.

Tiago walloped Nilson on the back, sending the smaller man reeling a few feet before they both laughed and took off after the group of male revelers—probably already half-high from the fumes given off by that stupid pipe.

Hmm. Matt's eyes *had* seemed different, the icy blue irises shoved aside, overtaken by the black centers. Of course that could have been caused by the unholy terror of finding himself standing next to her while the medicine man voiced his grim decrees.

She'd experienced a few misgivings herself.

One of the women headed her way with a spray of velvety purple flowers. Stevie tried to smile, but the growing knot in her stomach made it difficult.

'These are to help your marriage bed.' The woman ducked her head when a couple of giggles rang through the clearing.

'To help my…bed?'

Please, God, don't let anyone try to give me any feminine wisdom about my so-called wedding night.

'Yes, it counteracts the effects of the *ayahuasca*.'

Stevie frowned. 'Ay-a-skwa?'

More giggles.

'Yes, it is what your husband smokes from the *cachimba* pipe. A man cannot…perform his duties while under its influence.'

Her eyes widened. She assumed this 'duty' didn't involve winning an easy hand of poker. Lordy, how was she supposed to answer this one?

She didn't try. She simply held her hand out to accept the flowers the woman offered. The ones that promised to transform her new husband from impotent pothead into lover extraordinaire.

Except he'd said he hadn't inhaled. And if these flowers contained some kind of natural aphrodisiac, who knew what could happen? Even as she said it, she pictured a toxin working its way through her skin and reaching her bloodstream. Her fingers tingled, the sensation slowly spreading—moving up her arm in a delicious wave.

Stop it! It's just your imagination.

Her teeth came down on her lip. But what if it wasn't all in her mind? Matt had said the pipe contained a hallucinogen. So what did the flowers contain?

'Will they make me sick?'

The woman gave a smile filled with secrets. 'No. They will make you happy. More than you dreamed possible.'

The tingle spread to her chest, her nipples tightening under the onslaught, before moving to her abdomen and then lower.

She snatched open her hand, sending the flowers tumbling to the ground.

The woman simply scooped them back up and held them out.

Her brain tripped into action, hoping to find a way to refuse to touch them again. How humiliating would it be for Matt to come to the tent and find her all hot and needy, unable to fight her own impulses. 'I—ah...'

'She is shy,' the woman explained to those around her, with a soft laugh. 'That is okay, *doutora*. I will place them on the bed for you.'

'Thank you.' Her breath exited on a relieved hiss. Let them all believe she was embarrassed. Better than having them realize the truth. That she'd suddenly pictured those sensual petals scattered over their bed and her lying among them. Naked. Waiting for Matt's arrival—performance-impaired or not.

Excusing herself, she went to check on Belini and the new baby. She found them both asleep, the woman's mother dozing on a mat nearby. How precious that tiny baby looked sprawled across Belini's chest, the girl's hand securing her tiny charge. She could understand now why Matt had seemed indifferent as to whether the baby lived or died in the beginning. It was a defense mechanism to help him cope with the tragedy of his past.

She moved closer, placing her palm carefully on the woman's forehead, feeling for fever. Cool and dry.

A good sign. Her fingers moved to the baby's back. Also cool, the infant's breathing remained slow and steady. As she watched, the tiny mouth puckered, lips moving in rhythmic twitches.

Nursing in his sleep. Another positive sign.

As if sensing the slightest shifting of her child's weight, Belini's lids parted, blinking sleepily. When she saw Stevie standing there, her brows came together. 'The baby, he is okay?'

'Oh, yes, he's perfect.'

She knelt down next to the young mother and took one of her hands. 'How do you feel?'

'Better. Still weak, but better.'

'That's normal. You need to get a lot of rest.'

Her mother's voice came from nearby. 'I will help her.'

'I'm glad,' said Stevie, who found herself missing her own mother all of a sudden. 'Well, I just wanted to make sure you were okay. I'll let you sleep.'

Belini nodded. 'Thank you. For everything.'

As Stevie ducked out of the tent, she ran smack dab into a hard masculine chest.

Matt.

Large hands came out to steady her, holding her against his body, while the scent of some exotic smoke drifted from his skin…his clothing.

Ayahuasca. Viagra's biggest foe.

She swallowed. Except Matt didn't appear to need a little blue pill. Or a magic purple flower. The man was doing fine all by himself.

His voice rumbled over her head, the low, sexy tones winding around her like silk threads. 'I've been looking for you.'

'You have?'

'Umm-hmm.'

The hand on her back shifted an inch or two, and it took the shock of warm skin-on-skin contact to remind her of the serious lack of fabric across that area of her body.

'May I ask you a question?' he asked, as if he hadn't noticed the wave of heat that scorched through her.

'Q-question?' Yikes. Was it one she could answer without making a fool of herself? 'Is it personal?'

'Yes. Very.' His chin came to rest on her hair, and something in her melted, her body swaying a little closer to catch more of that hypnotic scent.

'What is it?'

'The flower petals in our hut.' The words carried a strange intensity. 'Who scattered them on the bed? You…or someone else?'

CHAPTER THIRTEEN

WHY had he asked her about the flowers? Maybe he'd gotten a few more whiffs of the *ayahuasca* than he'd realized. But when he'd entered the ceremonial hut expecting to find plain, bare-bones quarters and had encountered, instead, a lavish scene, he'd stopped in his tracks, his blood turning to sludge in his veins.

Baskets of fruit and bread lay scattered on oil-rubbed tables of varying heights. An offering to the gods? Or a gift for the lucky couple?

He'd glanced to the side, following a trail of light. Hundreds of natural candles surrounded a creamy white hammock, whose intricately braided fringe brushed the ground. The flickering glow bathed the bed in mystery. Intimacy.

And those petals.

Everywhere.

He found himself yearning for something that had nothing to do with breathing a potent drug and everything to do with the night and the woman now in his arms.

Except she was fidgeting.

'I…no, er, I had nothing to do with them. I think one of the women must have put them there.'

He blinked, his common sense returning with a bump. He'd hoped…

Nothing. He'd hoped nothing.

Matt dropped his arms and took a step back. Stevie's cheeks had turned the color of a fine Pinot Noir. And she wouldn't meet his eyes.

Her teeth came down on her lip. 'I don't think either of us should touch them.'

'Touch who? The women?' He had no idea what she was talking about. And this night was heading to hell in a hand basket.

'No. The flowers.' Her glance stayed on the ground in front of her. 'I think they might be spiked.'

He waited for a second, but she didn't seem in a hurry to explain herself. 'You think they're what?'

'Spiked. You know, with a drug. Like the pipe.'

'What gave you that idea?'

Stevie's face flamed even darker, her hands twisting in front of her. 'I mean, I don't have *firsthand* knowledge of what they might do…or anything.' An awkward pause ensued, then she blurted out, 'The women said it would counteract the pipe.'

'The *ayahuasca*?'

She nodded.

'So if I were under its influence, which I'm not—' although he was beginning to have some serious doubts on that front '—then the flowers would help me do what?'

It hit him. Too many tokes on the pipe, and he'd be down for the count. On his wedding night.

Something about the whole ludicrous situation—the wedding in their honor, his pierced ear, the *ayahuasca,* an aphrodisiacal flower flung across his bed—struck him the wrong way and he started laughing.

'What's so funny?' Stevie demanded, her brows coming together.

He cleared his throat, getting himself under control with some effort. Maybe he should try to lighten the atmosphere a little. 'Are you sure you didn't touch those flowers? Maybe I should take your pulse.'

Her eyes widened, and she stumbled back a step. 'That's ridiculous.'

He suddenly realized why she was so embarrassed and flustered. She *had* touched the flowers, and they'd affected her in some way. He wanted to drop his gaze and see if he could note any changes. He was a doctor, after all. He should examine her medically.

Right.

'It's okay, Stevie. No harm done.'

'Of course not.' Her eyes met his for the first time since they'd run into each other. 'But we need to get them out of that room. Just in case.'

He forced his lips not to lift. 'We'll sweep them onto the floor with a leaf. It'll be fine.'

Matt's smile quickly faded at the thought of them in that tent. Alone. With 'spiked' flowers.

Flowers or no flowers, spending the night with her would be like walking through a pit of glowing coals.

Painful. And not just for his feet.

Several hours later, he was still awake. From across the darkened hut came the slow, steady sound of Stevie's breathing. It mingled with the hum of the jungle just beyond the mud walls of the simple dwelling.

He looped his hands behind his head and tried to make out the thatching of the tiny hut's roof. With the candles snuffed out, it was too dark to see anything more than shadows. This particular hut had been made for guests and weddings, so the weave was tighter than most of the other dwellings. Not a single shaft of moonlight made it through.

It should be a blessing that he couldn't see her sleeping.

But somehow the murky interior just fed his imagination all the more, and he was afraid when he did fall asleep, his dreams would take up where his thoughts left off.

If there was a hell, it couldn't be much worse than this. He wasn't even touching her, but he could feel the softness of her skin beneath his hands, catch the fragrant scent from her hair as she turned her head to smile at him. See the growing need in her eyes...

And there you had it. Pathetic lust from a pathetic, lonely man who should have better things to do.

Like check on his patients.

Which was what he intended to do. Then he'd go and spend the rest of the night on the boat. In his own bed.

Hauling himself to his feet, he couldn't resist creeping closer to the double-sized hammock where Stevie lay. Just to make sure she was okay.

She was. He could barely make out her peaceful features in the dark, softened by the filmy netting that covered her sleeping area.

He closed a tiny gap that had opened in the mosquito netting, before turning and heading out the door, hoping no one spotted him as he made his rounds across the village. Scraping the hair off his forehead, his wrist brushed something hard in the process. The bead in his ear.

Proof he was a man.

Absurd.

And yet Stevie had leapt to her feet, willing to take his punishment for him. Something about that had touched him deeply. In a spot that hadn't been touched since…Vickie

He shut his eyes. He was fast approaching a line he'd drawn in the sand four years ago. One he'd sworn he'd never cross again.

The quiet tones of Vickie's voice echoed in his head, whispering that it was okay to let go. It was time.

No. It wasn't about letting go. It was about the whole lifestyle. About making choices for himself that didn't involve putting another person at risk. Matt intended to keep things the way they were.

He'd been alone since his wife's death. And unless he wanted to give up helping these people, that's the way it had to stay.

When he got back to the boat, he unlocked the door to the exam room and took down the medical reference. Maybe he needed to remind himself what could happen when you gave in to selfishness.

Opening the book to the section on dengue, he touched a finger to his wife's flowing handwriting, his eyes misting. He blinked to clear them and forced himself to read. To keep reading, entry by painful entry.

But as he got to the last line, Vickie's gentle voice was right there.

Reminding him that he had a new wife now. And that he'd better not blow his chance.

Warm fingers touched her cheek. 'Wake up, sleepyhead. Time to rise and shine.'

Stevie wrinkled her nose. It was much too early to be morning already. Besides, she'd been up half the night, waiting for Matt to come back from wherever he'd gone.

But he hadn't.

Until now.

Her lids parted, and she encountered Matt's blue eyes, now crinkling at the corners. Laughing at her.

Oh, God, she must look a wreck, while he looked…

Amazing. Good enough to eat, piece by gorgeous piece.

Dark hair, slicked back off his broad forehead, was damp from a recent shower. The spicy scent of soap fused with the woodsy fragrance of nearby cooking fires. Once the mixture hit her nostrils, she had to force herself not to breathe it deep into her lungs.

She sat up in a rush, running trembling fingers through her hair before yanking the whole mass back and tying it into a knot. She willed him to leave until she could at least wash her face and brush her teeth.

Crouched down beside her, he seemed in no hurry to move away. 'How'd you sleep?'

Swallowing, she pulled her gaze from his only to spy the discarded remains of the flower petals on the ground. Time to lie. 'I slept just fine, thanks. How about you?'

'Passable.'

Okay, so that made two of them who were spinning wild tales of fiction, because he'd never come back to their hut last night.

Unless he'd slept in someone else's.

A lump clogged her throat. For all she knew, he had a woman in each village waiting to satisfy his every need. Just like her ex-fiancé's lover had been.

She could have sworn Matt was different than Michael. Loyal.

He'd been close to kissing her last night as they'd stood in front of Belini's hut. Until she'd opened her big mouth and somehow killed the mood.

Which was a good thing, right? Especially since she had no idea where he'd gone after he'd snuck out of their room.

Somehow, though, with Matt still kneeling beneath her stretch of mosquito netting, she felt a loss she didn't want to examine.

Dropping her hands to her lap, she racked her brain for something else to say, but he beat her to the punch. 'Belini's better. I checked on her this morning. And the other patients are getting stronger. We should be able leave within the next day or two.'

'Really? You think the worst has passed?'

A glimpse of something resembling sorrow flashed through his eyes and was gone. 'I hope so.'

'Me too.' She caught sight of his earring and winced before reaching up to touch the bead. 'Speaking of the worst being past, how's your ear doing?'

'Good. I doused it with alcohol this morning and...' His words faded away. He reached up to grab her wrist and turned it upside down.

'Hey, what are you—?'

'Hold still.' He stared at her arm, tilting it to and fro before rubbing his thumb over the tender flesh of her forearm.

Her stomach flipped as the calloused pad did wonky things to her insides.

She had no idea what he was doing. But she liked it. She had no intention of stopping him.

Had the man been rolling in those flower petals while she wasn't looking? If so, she wasn't going to complain. He leaned closer to her arm, and her lips parted as she wondered if he was going to kiss it.

'Damn it to hell,' he whispered.

Taken aback by the rough words, she blinked.

He hadn't moved from where he knelt, but the stroking had stopped. It was as if he were paralyzed in that one spot, unable to move.

'Matt? What is it?' He was blocking her view, so she couldn't see what he was so upset about. Was her arm smeared with dirt? Blood?

At her words, he sat up straight, and her limb came into view.

She dragged her eyes from his face and peered at her arm, trying to focus. What was going on?

When his thumb rubbed the spot again, she realized it was a bit itchy, like she'd been bitten…

Dread circled her insides, spinning an icy web of fear. She was in a village surrounded by dengue fever patients. And rising on her arm, looking angrier by the second, was a mosquito bite.

CHAPTER FOURTEEN

'WE DON'T even know if it was an *Aedes Aegypti* mosquito. It could have been one of any number of species.'

The stiff set of his lips didn't soften. 'It doesn't matter. We're leaving. Now.'

Standing on the deck of the medical boat, she'd been trying to get through to him for the last hour. 'Matt, be reasonable. A hospital can't do anything for me unless I'm symptomatic. So even if the bite is from a dengue carrier, the incubation period can be up to fourteen days. We'll have finished treating all the patients in the village by that time.'

A muscle worked in his jaw. 'Median incubation is four to eight days.'

'Still plenty of time. I'll take precautions not to spread it to anyone else.'

'It's not anyone else I'm worried about.' His eyes closed before reopening and fixing her with an angry glare. 'Why weren't you wearing repellent?' He dragged a hand through his hair.

'I did! At least during the day, but I don't like the stickiness or the smell at night. Besides, I had the net around the bed.'

'And you'd left a huge gap in the seam. I had to pull it closed before I went out to check on our patients.'

He was being absurd. 'The gap wasn't big. It was tiny. I didn't even see it until you—'

'You were awake?'

She licked her lips, realizing she'd been found out. 'Yes.'

'Why didn't you say something?'

She shrugged. 'What was I supposed to say?'

There was no way either of them could answer that, and she knew it.

'We should have left when the medicine man issued his warning. Or when I knew Belini was improving. Going through with the celebration last night was a mistake.'

'There was no choice. Belini could have died during labor. Her baby could have died. Midwives can't perform emergency surgery.'

He swore again. 'Do you know what could happen if you contract this?'

'Yes.' Wanting to reassure him, she touched his arm. 'I promise you, I'm not taking this lightly. I know what this disease can do. I've seen it.'

'So have I.'

'Oh, Matt, I know you have. And I hate that I'm the reason those terrible memories are resurfacing.' Her eyes moistened. 'But I want to stay. I *need* to stay. Just for a few more days. Please let me finish this.'

He stared at her for several long minutes, and then his attention shifted to her arm, which he'd insisted on slathering with antibiotic cream and covering with a waterproof bandage. Gripping her hand, he shook his head. 'I don't like this.'

'As soon as the last of our patients is in the clear, we'll leave. I promise.'

'This is all just so…' Unexpectedly, his palm cupped the back of her neck, his fingers warm and gentle as he gazed down at her. 'I owe you an apology.'

Expecting yet another argument, his words took her by surprise. 'W-what?'

He smiled. 'When you first showed up at the airport, I thought you were another down-on-your-luck medical practitioner looking to get out of the rut of your particular specialty. That you wanted to do something adventurous. Prove yourself to the world. But you're not just another washed-up doc, are you?' With gentle pressure from his hand, he drew her closer. 'You're the real deal. You're more interested in these people than you are in yourself.'

Guilt hit, hard and swift. If he only knew the real reason she'd come, he'd know she was a fraud. She *had* come here out of self-ish motives. After all, what could be more selfish than taking a job to get away from a cheating fiancé? From a hospital that no longer wanted you?

But something had changed over the course of the last two weeks. She'd grown to love the people of these villages. It was like a part of her she hadn't known was missing had suddenly dropped into place. A perfect fit.

And Matt...

Was something she didn't dare think about right now. Not when he spoke to her with something akin to admiration in his voice. An admiration which made her feel...valued. Special. Things she hadn't felt in a very long time. And there was more. Something lurked behind his eyes. A tenderness she didn't dare try to decipher.

She swallowed. 'I'm not as noble as you're making me out to be.'

'Are any of us?' He glanced around as if making sure no one would overhear them and lowered his voice. 'When I saw that bite, I—'

'I know.' The shadows in his eyes were almost more than she could bear. He was so close, and both of them were scared, lonely and hurting, right now. What would it matter in all eternity if she just leaned forward and...?

Before she realized what she was doing, she'd closed the two-inch gap that lay between them and touched her lips to his. He flinched, whether in surprise or rejection she wasn't sure. And she didn't have time to figure it out because a second later his palms slid up her arms, then cupped her cheeks. Tilting his head, he kissed her back, stepping closer until she felt the hard press of his chest against her breasts. Her nipples reacted immediately. Tightening with need.

Heaven. This was heaven. As was the firm, insistent pressure of his lips. The moist touch of his tongue as it slid along the seam of her mouth.

'*Mmm.*'

Okay, so she hadn't meant to say that aloud, but so what? And Matt didn't seem to mind, if the hand now applying steady pressure to the small of her back was any indication.

And, oh, yeah, there was that reminder that this man could rise to any occasion. She inched closer, relishing the shudder that rippled through his chest when she angled her hips just so.

She opened her mouth to let him in, and he didn't waste any time. A low growl rose in his throat as his tongue slid against hers, pressing hard and deep. A hand to the back of her head held her in place, not giving her a chance to retreat. As if she would.

Having this man drive her crazy was something she could get used to. So used to.

His thrusts held a desperation that intoxicated her—a focused intensity that weakened her knees and robbed her lungs of breath. He seemed to know exactly what course he was setting, and Stevie had no intention of trying to divert him from it.

Fisting her hands in his shirt, she fought to keep her balance as she maneuvered a set of emotional rapids, navigating around treacherous stretches of whitewater. One wrong move, and she'd slip beneath the surface.

Who cared?

Incredible. Maddening. That's what this was. And her need grew stronger with each heated stroke of his tongue.

Even with Michael—during their most intimate lovemaking—she hadn't experienced anything like this.

Never this amalgamation of ecstasy and dread that terrified her, yet made her crave more of the same.

His mouth left hers and trailed slow moist kisses down her neck. She shivered, his name coming out as a husky moan she couldn't contain.

He stopped, his lips still pressed to her throat.

She waited for him to continue, and although his breath rasped in and out as if he'd just run a marathon, he didn't move.

No!

He couldn't mean to stop. Not now. Not when everything inside of her screamed for him to lay her down on the deck and finish what he'd started.

What *she'd* started. Her eyes fluttered open as the gravity of what she'd done filtered through her foggy brain.

'I don't have anything on board.' The whispered phrase left a moist imprint on her flesh.

'Anything?' What was he talking about?

'Condoms. The ones in the first aid kit have been around forever. They're too old to be safe.'

'Oh.' Her face heated, then she remembered something. 'What about the ones in the health kits?'

'Gone. Tiago passed the last of them out to the villagers two days ago.' He paused. 'Are you protected?'

She hadn't exactly planned on having sex as she traveled down the Amazon, since she thought she'd be working with Tracy. And a two-year supply of the Pill seemed like one more thing to have to drag around with her and remember to take.

Besides. There was the 'no planned sex' thing.

'No. I'm not.' The words came out as a croak.

He raised his head to look down at her before pressing his forehead to hers. 'God. Sorry.'

For what? Being out of condoms? That he was having to stop? Just what the hell was he sorry for?

'It's nothing,' she forced herself to say.

The hands on her arms tightened, before he released the pressure. Released her. 'Right. Nothing.'

She tried to detect regret in his words, but his tone was strangely void of emotion. 'We're under a lot of stress—the outbreak…the wedding celebration.' She rubbed her bandaged arm. 'We weren't thinking rationally.'

'And now we are.'

She jerked her glance to his face. He might be, but she wasn't so sure about herself. 'Of course.'

He was silent for several long seconds, then he turned his back to her and looked out over the *Rio Preto*. When his voice came, it was firm. No sign of any of the turmoil she was battling inside. 'You have four days. Then we leave.'

Four days later, Stevie had no signs of dengue, neither were there any new cases in the village. The outbreak was over. At least for the moment. And hell if Stevie hadn't somehow talked him into continuing on to their next planned stop. As if she was certain she was in no danger from the illness.

Or from him.

He'd expected her to at least want to go back to Coari to be examined at one of the clinics. And he'd have used that time to make a quick run to the nearest *farmácia*.

Just in case.

But Stevie seemed sure of her own ability to resist temptation. To resist him.

That very thought made him want to growl a few choice words into the warm breeze. He settled for mouthing them under his breath.

'You are okay, Mateus?' Tiago's voice came from beside him on deck.

'Fine.'

'Why, then, are you still sleeping in the dining hall? Did you fight with Miss Stevie?'

His fingers tightened on the rail. 'No, I did not fight with Miss Stevie.' Whose bright idea had it been to allow the village to throw them an honorary wedding ceremony? He should set his crew members straight and tell them the ceremony had been a fraud, but he was afraid word might make its way back to Belini's village and offend the chief. So he kept his mouth shut.

'Then why—?'

Matt held up his hand to stave off the question. 'I didn't need any distractions, especially now.'

'Ah, I see.' The other man smiled. 'She is a very beautiful woman, no?'

His attention jerked to Tiago's face, a strange wave of anger and possessiveness coursing through him. 'Yes. As is your own wife.'

'Of course. I didn't mean to offend.' There was nothing in his crew member's demeanor that indicated he was interested in Stevie. Which made Matt feel like a first-class cad.

'You didn't offend me. I'm just worried.' He decided to tell

Tiago part of the reason for that worry. 'She was bitten back at the village.'

'Bitten?' His eyes widened. 'By a mosquito? You think she might catch the sickness?'

'No.' But even he could hear the doubt behind his negation. And if he could, then Tiago definitely heard it.

Sure enough, the man crossed himself as if warding off evil. 'Surely God would not see fit to take two...'

Probably realizing he'd said way too much, Tiago allowed his words to fade away, but Matt could fill in the rest of the sentence: Surely God wouldn't see fit to take two of Matt's wives.

That was exactly the reason they should turn this boat around and head in the opposite direction.

Except he'd promised Stevie he'd trust her judgement.

Like he had Vickie's?

She's not really your wife, Matt. She's a colleague, nothing more.

Even as he thought the words, his fingers went to the bead in his left ear.

'She will not contract the illness. Have faith.' Tiago gave his shoulder a quick squeeze before he left to go about his work.

Have faith.

At one time those words would have awoken something within him. But not any more. His faith had failed him before. He wasn't sure he could risk his heart—or Stevie's—to the whims of a silent deity.

Not this time. Because the second she'd kissed him while standing on that deck four days ago something inside him had shifted.

First in his body. And then in his heart.

Until he could figure out how to crush the emotion...or at least hold it at bay...he needed to make sure he didn't put her in any more danger.

CHAPTER FIFTEEN

'I TOLD you, I'm not leaving. I signed on for two years, remember?'

Stevie kept her eyes on the small boy she was treating, smearing antibiotic lotion onto the child's cut and reverting back to Portuguese. 'See there? It didn't hurt at all.'

Even though she hadn't glanced at Matt, she could feel his glare searing the back of her white T-shirt.

'It's the easiest solution. The villagers at Tupari will continue to think we're married, even if you return to the States. So far none of the other villages have questioned your presence or our relationship. And with you gone, there'll be no need for the crew to wonder whether or not that wedding ceremony was the real thing or not.'

She rolled her eyes as she sent her patient on his way. It wasn't like Matt had gone to great lengths to fool anyone. He was still sleeping in the dining hall. They hadn't touched since that fiasco of a kiss on the deck a week ago. 'All we have to do is tell them the truth.'

He moved around to stand in front of her where he towered over her. She suddenly regretted her precarious perch on the log, but she'd wanted to be at eye level with the child she'd been treating. She'd had no idea Matt would bring up this subject.

Again.

Her mosquito bite had faded to a tiny bruise, and there'd been no signs of illness. Eleven days and counting. In another three or four, it would be safe to assume she was out of the woods.

At least as far as Dengue was concerned.

'I didn't want Nilson or Tiago to say anything to the villagers. Neither the medicine man nor the chief would take kindly to being lied to.'

'I know how much of a hardship all of this has been for you.' The waspish words were out before she could stop them. She stood, just to show him she wasn't afraid of him. Or maybe to show herself.

They'd set up a makeshift clinic in the large cooking area of the village they were currently visiting, a place where anyone who needed medical attention could find them. The neat dirt clearing was the size of a basketball court, and the true heart of the tribe. With people constantly traipsed through the clearing on their way to one place or another, it made having this kind of discussion difficult, which was why they'd switched to English. To Stevie, it seemed rude, like they were whispering secrets about those around them.

Tiago and Nilson were busy scrubbing down the deck of the *Projeto Vida*, so they were safely out of earshot. The only witnesses to their argument were a few women who knelt a short distance away, beating cassava roots that would later be turned into a type of flour. Without special attention to preparation, the roots contained a toxin powerful enough to kill. Her and Matt's raised voices had piqued the interest of the small group, causing a couple of the women to glance their way. Stevie balked at saying anything else, even in English.

'Can we continue this discussion another time?' She nodded toward the women. 'They need to concentrate on what they're doing. I, for one, prefer not to be the cause of the whole tribe dying of cyanide poisoning.'

Matt's glance flicked to the group. 'Let's go down by the river.'

Before she had a chance to respond, a woman came up to them, holding a baby in her arms. The worry on her face caught Stevie's attention immediately, as did the infant's thin cries. Stroking the baby's cheek, Stevie tried to soothe the child while gauging the temperature and moisture level of her skin. 'Is your baby sick?'

'Yes. She cries and refuses to nurse. And today she began to vomit.'

Matt moved forward and eased the swaddling back from the baby's forehead. 'No fever.' He glanced at the mother. 'When was she born?'

'Two days ago.'

Stevie held out her arms, silently asking to hold the child. The mother hesitated, glancing from one to the other.

'It's okay,' Stevie said. 'I just want to look at her. I promise I'll give her back.'

Once the child was in her arms, she rocked her gently, a frightening sense of déjà vu shooting through her as the baby refused to be comforted. Just a few months ago she'd held an infant very similar to this one and listened to the anguished pleas of his parents as they'd begged her to save their child. In New York, Stevie had had access to the best equipment modern medicine could buy. The only thing she'd lacked had been the hospital's permission to operate. This time no hospital stood in her way, but the boat had rudimentary facilities and if the problem was serious...

Was one situation any better than the other?

She crushed the painful memory and glanced at Matt. 'Do we examine her here or on the boat?'

'Let's start here.' He motioned toward the stool. 'You can lay her across your lap and undress her in her mother's presence.'

While Matt asked some questions, Stevie listened with half an ear as she unwrapped the blanket. The first thing she did was check the wadding between the baby's legs. Slightly wet, but no sign of feces.

Next, she used her index finger to compress the skin on the baby's arm and examine the color. Normal and pink. No sign of jaundice or compromised blood flow. Closing her eyes, she sent up a quick prayer of thanks.

She continued down her mental checklist, her glance traveling down the baby's chest and over the abdomen.

Distended.

Palpating lightly, she encountered firm coils of bowel on the left side. Possible obstruction. She glanced up at the mother.

'Has she had a bowel movement?' she asked in Portuguese.

The mother tilted her head. 'I do not understand.'

Matt changed the wording and re-asked the question.

'No,' the mother said. 'There's been nothing.'

She switched to English. 'I want to take her aboard. I think she may have an obstruction.'

Half expecting Matt to interfere or try to take over the case, he did neither. 'How do you want to handle it?'

'If she hasn't passed meconium yet, there could be a plug. A simple saline enema could resolve the problem. If not, we'll have to look at some more serious possibilities.'

'Okay. Let's do it.'

Her eyes widened. And that was it? No arguments? No waffling? She waited a few seconds just in case, but nothing came. He was letting her follow her instincts. So different than Michael's reaction would have been.

Carefully rewrapping the infant, she stood and tucked the baby against her shoulder, turning to explain the situation to the mother. 'Can we take her on the boat? You can come with us.'

'You will not hurt her?'

'No, I promise. I'm hoping she'll feel better very soon.'

The whole process took less time than Stevie expected. Within thirty minutes, just as she'd hoped, the warm saline did the trick.

'Thank God,' she breathed to herself.

Matt, who'd stayed by her side throughout the procedure, laid a hand on her shoulder, giving it a quick squeeze. 'Good work. You were right.'

The warmth of his hand, along with his easy praise, sent a shiver of longing through her. She wanted to stay right here and relish this moment—to take it deep into her heart. But she still had her patient to care for.

Quickly cleaning the baby, she leaned down to kiss her tiny cheek. 'You're going to be just fine. Grow up big and strong for me, okay?'

As if understanding exactly what Stevie said, the child scrunched up her face and let out a cry. Not of pain this time. But if Stevie was interpreting the sound correctly, she was hungry.

Famished.

She handed the baby to her mother, who put her to her breast. Rooting around for a second, the infant soon found her target and latched on. Sounds of vigorous nursing filled the air around them.

'She eats.' The mother's eyes met hers. 'If you had not been here to help...' Her voice trailed away, and she stroked her daughter's head.

Matt left the room, shutting the door with a quiet click. As much as she wanted to follow him, she knew she had to make sure the baby and her mother were going to be okay. She waited for the infant to finish feeding, then checked her over once again. The baby's abdomen had already lost much of its bloated appearance. 'I'll have Tiago take you back to shore, but I'd like to check her again tomorrow. Make sure you find me.'

'Yes, I will.'

As soon as the dinghy left for shore, Stevie went looking for Matt. Probably not a wise move, but knowing his wife had been pregnant when she'd died changed things. Once she knew he was okay, she'd go back to her cabin and try to get some sleep.

She found him in the dining room, hunched over the table. His hammock was already strung up for the night, but he was still dressed. He looked up as soon as she entered, and the question she'd been about to ask died in her throat.

His face...dear Lord, *his face.* The man was in agony.

She hurried over to him. 'What is it? Your neck?'

'I'm fine.' He stood, and only then did she notice the open medical reference on the tabletop. At the sight of familiar slanting handwriting, her heart sank. She hadn't noticed the book's absence from the shelf in the infirmary as she'd worked on the baby.

'Oh, Matt. Don't do this to yourself.'

He shook off her words with an irritated lift of his left shoulder. 'What I'm *doing* is my job.'

'And yet you want to send me away and keep me from doing mine.' She motioned to the book. 'It all makes sense now. I think by reminding yourself of the terrible things that happened to your wife, it'll be easier to force me to leave.'

She took a step forward, tilting her face until she saw the brilliant blue of his eyes. Those eyes that made her insides quake every time they met hers. 'Don't you see, Matt? I can be an asset to your work. There may be women in some of the villages who won't feel comfortable talking to a man, but they'd be okay sharing personal health problems with me. Yes, the conditions on the boat are difficult, given the space constraints, but we can make it work. Can't you see the benefit of having both a man and a woman on the team?'

'You're making a good argument, but—'

'But nothing. I'm right and you know it. I've yet to hear you say anything that convinces me otherwise.'

'It's not that I don't think you're capable.' A muscle worked in his jaw. 'You've proven time and time again that you are. But if something happened…I don't want to be responsible.'

'Happened. You mean to me?'

He nodded.

Stevie put her hand on his forearm, the action bringing her a step closer. Something told her his need to get rid of her went far deeper than he was letting on. 'What happened to your wife wasn't your fault, Matt. As awful as it was, she chose to be here. With you. It's what she wanted.'

The muscles under her hand bunched until they became a solid mass, hard and unyielding. 'I think you should leave my wife out of this.'

'Someone needs to make you see the truth.' She released his arm so she could slide her fingers down the rigid line of flesh in his neck. 'The problem with your back, did it begin after your wife died?'

'None of this is any of your business.' He reached back and gripped her wrist, pulling it away from him.

Before he could drop her hand, she twined her fingers around his and held on. 'You want to get rid of me because of what happened to your wife. I think that makes it my business.'

'No. It doesn't.' Despite his words, he didn't walk away from her, didn't wrench his hand from hers. But there was an awful despair in his eyes that tore at her. He'd lost his wife and baby to a disease that claimed lives every year along the Amazon. What right did she have to minimize what he'd gone through?

None.

But she wished with all her might she could make his pain go away. That when he looked at her he didn't see a potential disaster, but a potential...

Her lips parted. Oh, God. What was she thinking?

This was a man who'd never gotten over the loss of his wife. A man who might never look at a woman and see anything other than heartache. Why else would he insulate himself from any female contact, outside those he treated in the villages?

She was a fool to think that would ever change.

That she would even *want* it to change. Hadn't she already slogged through one disastrous relationship and come through on the losing end? Did she really want to jump into one she knew from the onset was doomed?

No.

Yes.

'Stevie?'

Her eyes watered unexpectedly, and she tried to blink away the moisture, but it was too late. The second her lids slammed shut, two tears squeezed from between them and tumbled down her cheeks.

'Oh, hell.' He wrapped an arm around her and pulled her against him, until her cheek was resting against his chest. She could hear the thunderous beat of his heart as it pumped blood through his body, the sound sure and solid beneath her ear. The sensation made her even weepier, and she gritted her teeth to force the tears down her throat.

His fingers filtered through her hair, until he reached her scalp and rubbed in soothing circles. 'I don't know why I said that. You're right. None of this is your fault. And it's not really why I've been trying to find a replacement.' His voice rumbled beneath her cheek.

'Why are you, then?'

His fingers paused for a moment, before taking up where they'd left off. 'You don't want to know.'

She tilted her head to look up at him, but only got a close-up view of the bottom of his chin. There was a small scar she'd never noticed before. She longed to touch it, but didn't dare. 'I do want to know.'

'Trust me on this one.'

'If knowing will help me change your mind...'

'It would. That's what I'm afraid of.'

'I don't understand. What are you afraid of?'

His chin moved to and fro as he shook his head. 'I can't tell you.'

'Then show me. Help me understand.' Her hand went to his face, her thumb tracing the sharp angle of his cheekbone.

'Don't.' The low rasp of his voice slid through her like silk.

The whole world shifted. The solid press of his body was no longer comforting, but deadly. Her brain searched frantically for something that would anchor her to reality, but found nothing but longing.

Need.

Aware she was treading on dangerous ground, she touched her lips to the scar on his chin. 'Where did you get this?' she whispered.

'What?' The fingers in her hair had long ceased their exploration and lay tense and still against her head.

'Your scar. I never noticed it before.'

'Surfboard.'

Stevie took a moment to digest this. The man who was afraid to live his life had once braved ocean waves? 'You used to surf?'

'No. A roommate left his board near the door of our dorm room. I tripped over it in the dark, and it caught me in the chin. Six stitches.'

She smiled. 'Ouch.'

'Stevie?'

'Yes?'

'I think you should move away before I do something we'll both regret.'

Her heart tripped a couple of beats. 'Are you sure about that?'

'That I'll do something I'll regret?'

'No. Are you sure we'd *both* regret it?'

His fingers fisted in her hair and used gentle pressure to tilt her head back. 'Are you saying you wouldn't?'

She licked her lips. 'Are you saying you would?'

He slowly shook his head back and forth. 'No.'

'Then, if neither of us would regret it...'

His head lowered until his mouth was a prayer away from hers. And she was praying like mad.

'Not here,' he muttered.

He took hold of her hand and led her back to the bedroom, closing the door with a click.

With her heart hammering in her chest, she pressed her back against the solid wooden surface.

Please don't back out this time.

He answered her silent plea by propping a hand on either side of her head, and without touching her anywhere else leaned in and placed a hard kiss on her mouth. She immediately tried to wiggle closer, only to have him swear and lean his forehead against hers.

'Damn. No protection, remember?'

Stevie should care. Really she should. But at the moment all she wanted was his mouth back on hers. The kiss had been way too short and intoxicating to end so quickly. She'd worry about the rest later.

'Tiago's married, isn't he? I saw a ring. Maybe he has something.'

'He does have something: five kids.' Matt gave a soft laugh.

'Oh.'

'Yeah. Oh.'

But instead of moving away from her, he edged closer, sliding his cheek across hers, the slight rasp of his beard sending a needy shiver through her.

'Do you trust me?' His lips brushed the sensitive flesh of her ear with each word.

The breath whooshed from her lungs, and she had to replace it before she could manage to answer. 'Yes.'

'I won't put you at risk. I promise.'

The only thing at risk right now was him if he didn't put his mouth back on hers immediately. 'Stop talking,' she ordered.

'So bossy.' His low laugh softened the words, while his hands slid down her arms until they reached her hips. Fingers biting into her flesh, he brought her against him, until she felt each hard inch of him.

Heavens. There was more of him than she'd expected.

Wrapping her arms around his neck, she stretched up on tiptoe, hoping to find his lips, but he leaned just out of reach. The tantalizing slope of his mouth shifted into a crooked grin. 'Not until you say something.'

'What?'

'Say you like it when I kiss you.'

'You know I do.' Her fingers pushed into his hair, hoping to force his head down, but it was like trying to drag a two-hundred-pound anchor across the ocean floor. Impossible.

'I don't know.' He moved an inch closer until their breaths met. Mingled. 'So say it.'

'Matt, please.'

'Uh-uh. Say the words.'

'I like it.'

'You like what?'

She squirmed against him, an answering smile coming over her when a groan erupted from his throat. 'I like that I can make you do that.'

'Hell, woman. You have no idea what you might make me do if you keep that up.'

Her eyes widened. 'Oh.'

'Yeah. Oh.' He held her hips still. 'It's been a while.'

Leaning down, he tugged her lower lip between his teeth and

stroked his tongue across it, sending a wild electrical charge through her before he backed off again. She almost screamed with frustration, fisting her hands in his shirt and giving him a quick thump in the chest. 'Stop it.'

'Sorry. There are just so many delectable spots. I can't decide where to start.'

'Anywhere. Start anywhere. I don't care.' Neither did she care that the words came out a panted plea.

'In that case…' His nose brushed the line of her jaw and tipped her head to the side. 'I think I'll start here.'

He kissed her throat, his lips warm and sure. 'Your neck drives me crazy. So long. So delicate. You don't know how many times I've wanted to run my tongue along this line.' He demonstrated in slow motion, wringing a strangled moan from her.

'Or how many times I've wanted to bite you right here.' His teeth nipped at the joint between her shoulder and her throat and then stuck around to suckle the spot before moving an inch to the right and repeating the action.

Sweet heavens. She'd wanted him to shut up and kiss her, but the lush explicitness of his commentary made her imagination run wild. Her nipples tightened even as they wondered when he was going to include them in his little soliloquy.

As if privy to her thoughts, his hands slid beneath her shirt and swept over her ribcage until he reached her breasts, covering them with his palms.

She heard him suck down a breath. 'Damn. This should be illegal.'

'What should?'

'Going braless.' His thumbs scraped over her sensitive peaks, and her eyes fluttered closed at the raw sensations he sent spiraling through her belly. 'But I like it.'

He shoved her shirt up and over her head, tossing it to the side where it slid down the wall with a whisper of sound.

Her senses were running so hot that while the air around her must have been warm and balmy, the soft breeze that brushed against her torso seemed chilly. And empty.

She wasn't cold for long, because Matt's mouth soon took up

where his hands left off, tugging at one of her nipples and stroking it repeatedly with his tongue.

Whimpering with need, she burrowed her fingers into his hair and held him against her.

He obliged by biting down, and she arched against him, her legs threatening to give out when he held her captive with his teeth, lapping at the most sensitive spot with his tongue. A terrible, awful wave went through her, and she tugged at his hair, needing more from him, not wanting to wait another second. 'Matt.'

He answered by covering her lips with his, crowding her against the door with his body. Her tongue speared into his mouth, showing him the only way she knew how what she wanted from him. When his hands slid over her butt and cupped the backs of her thighs, it was as if they were of one mind. She parted her legs and allowed him to lift her onto his hips where that hard ridge of flesh hit just the right spot.

Something in the back of her mind registered that she still had on her slacks. Her panties. But he was pressing into her and releasing with rhythmic strokes, while she mimicked the timing with her tongue. No way was she going to stop and argue what now seemed like a minor point. There was plenty of time.

Plenty. Of…

Matt suddenly added another exquisite layer, sliding deeper between her thighs, her tortured flesh screaming *Yes!* when he picked up the pace, even as her mind warned her it was too soon. Too many clothes still lay between them. And, God, he was right there…pressing…grinding…groaning that it was okay…

Her head went back, mouth tearing from his as an orgasmic wave like nothing she'd ever encountered roared over her, tossing her end over end. She screamed, the sound impossible to contain, before his mouth covered hers again, trapping the remainder of the shriek. All the while, his body continued to move, not letting up until he'd wrung the very last spasm from her. She went limp in his arms, shaking as she held onto him for dear life.

He kissed her softly, again and again, murmuring how beautiful she was, how much he'd needed her to come for him.

Fragments of reality returned, a splinter here, a scrap there, taking over the mindless pleasure she'd just received. Her brain registered several things at once: the roughness of Matt's shirt against her sensitive nipples; the fact that she still had on most of her clothes; that he'd kept his word and not put her at risk.

And that he was still hard.

So very, very hard.

She blinked. Surely he'd already…

Her eyes met his, saw the stiff set of his mouth as he tried to smile at her, and she knew.

He hadn't.

'Matt. Put me down for a minute.'

He did, visibly wincing as her body skimmed over his.

This wouldn't do. Not at all. Stevie was all about fair play.

Okay, so that was a lie. The reality was that his still-raging hard-on was getting under her skin. All over again.

She slid her hands to the front of his jeans, searching for the button.

'Don't. We can't.'

A slow smile tilted her lips. '*We're* not. I am.'

The button on his jeans slid through the hole with a pop, and Matt shuddered as she tugged the zipper down his length.

'Hell, woman, if you keep doing that, I won't be able to stop.'

Sliding to her knees before him, she hauled his pants down in one quick motion, releasing him to her viewing pleasure. Her hand wrapped around him, and she leaned closer, watching his eyes darken as he realized what she was about to do. 'Well, now, Doctor. That's exactly what I'm counting on.'

CHAPTER SIXTEEN

MATT stared out over the dark, silent river, and though his feet remained anchored to the deck of the boat, the uneasy sensation that had kept him up most of the night persisted.

Something inside him was in danger of slipping beneath the surface of the *Rio Preto*—never to be seen again—drowning, held down by a piece of unbreakable cording. Even as he railed against his fate, he was powerless to fight it. Nearby lay more of the same strands, undulating to and fro, like slender filaments of seaweed just waiting to ensnare his foot if it ventured too close.

Stevie was still in her hammock as far as he knew. And he wasn't about to go in that room to wake her up. If he did, another treacherous strand would loop around him.

Even now he could feel the warm heat of her mouth as she'd enveloped him, her eyes never leaving his as she brought him to the edge of oblivion.

And hell if that memory wasn't enough to make him hard.

He gripped the handrail. Last night he'd miscalculated his willpower, and although they hadn't consummated the union—he knew himself well enough to know things weren't going to end there.

It was time to decide. He needed to do one of two things. Either pick up a package of condoms so he didn't have to wonder any longer what it would be like to slide into her depths and lose himself inside her. Or get Stevie off this boat and send her home before he got in even deeper. He cringed at the wording.

Just how strong was he? Could he send her away?

It was the smart thing to do.

But no one had ever said he always chose the wisest path. And it wasn't the first time a woman had swayed his decision.

Just look at what had happened to Vickie. He closed his eyes, his hand clenching the rail tighter. If they'd just gone back to the city when he'd wanted to, there was a good chance she and the baby would be alive today.

But they weren't. And Stevie was. Alive and healthy, and she'd come to Brazil for all the right reasons, unlike some of the doctors who had come through before her.

As if he'd summoned her, he sensed her come up behind him just before she appeared in his peripheral vision.

'You okay?' She stood alongside him at the edge of the deck.

Her question brought a quick smile to his face. He should be the one asking that, not her. He'd practically sent her crashing through the solid door of the bedroom last night. He'd noticed a bruise or two on her hips as she'd undressed, where his fingers had gripped her flesh. He'd fled the room soon afterwards.

'I'm fine.' He swallowed. 'About last night, I—'

'If you're going to apologize, save it.' She tossed her head, sending a couple of loose curls flipping over her shoulder. 'We're both adults. We both wanted what happened.'

Oh, he'd wanted a whole lot more than what they'd done, and he couldn't trust himself not to take it—all of it—which was why he'd turned around and headed back to Coari first thing that morning. Before he did something he really would regret.

'Okay. No apologies.'

She peered up at the sky and tilted her head. 'Wait. Aren't we headed in the wrong direction? I thought for sure I'd...persuaded you to keep me on. For a while at least.'

He frowned at her choice of words. Hopefully the persuasion she was referring to had to do with the pretty little speech she'd given in the dining room and not to what they'd done last night.

'We're out of health kits. I decided to go to Coari to pick up some supplies.'

It wasn't a lie. Not completely anyway. Belini's village had taken up a huge chunk of time. As soon as he made a decision about whether to keep Stevie on the team or drop her off once they arrived at the city, he'd head back down the river and make the rest of his stops.

'What about the baby? I told her I'd check on her today.'

'I saw Tiago when he came back to the boat. He said the baby had another bowel movement on the way to shore. He should be fine.'

'I'm so glad.' She paused. 'Since we're heading back, would it be possible to stop at Tupari? I'd like to say hello and check on Belini.'

'I'm sure things are fine. I can radio Tracy and ask if she's heard anything from the tribe.'

She frowned up at him. 'Surely we can spare a couple of hours. We haven't passed the village yet, have we?'

'No.' But he didn't want her stepping foot in Tupari as long there was the slightest possibility that any dengue infections were still active. She'd dodged the bullet this time. But what about the next?

Anger welled up inside him. *Send her home, then.*

If he couldn't separate his heart from his head, he needed to be man enough to do something about it. He couldn't continue to be paralyzed by fear. If that meant never working with another woman—which had been a decision Tracy had taken out of his hands this time—then he needed to make it clear he'd leave *Projeto Vida* if she went against him again.

'What are you thinking about?'

He shrugged. 'About how long it'll take to get back to the city.'

Laying a hand on his arm, she slid it down a few inches until her fingers encircled his wrist. 'Please. I'll never forgive myself if we pass by the village and something happens.'

The what-ifs worked their evil magic. Only this time he could do something about them, rather than let them play mind games on him. 'Fine. We'll stop. But only for an hour or two.'

'Thank you.' She smiled up at him, reaching on tiptoe and pressing her soft lips against his cheek. 'You won't regret it.'

He already did.

Nilson's voice came from behind him. 'Tiago just radioed. He's asking when you'll be back for him.'

'Back for him? I thought you said he came back aboard last night.' Stevie stared at Matt, her expression puzzled.

'He returned to the village early this morning. It's his tribe. His wife and children are there.'

'I didn't realize he was from one of the…' She tilted her head. 'Why didn't you wake me up?'

Not a chance. He'd been half-crazy at what he'd let himself do…at what he'd let Stevie do. He was afraid if he lay in that room with her until dawn, he'd finish things between them. So when he'd told Tiago he wanted to head back to Coari, his crew member had stared longingly at shore. Matt had realized that by cutting their visit short, Tiago's time with his family would also be cut short. So he'd told him to take a few days of vacation. The fact that there'd be one less person to chide Matt if he decided to leave Stevie behind hadn't played into his decision at all.

'It was early. I thought you'd like to sleep in for a change.' He turned to Nilson. 'Tell him I'm not sure of the exact date. But I'll radio a few days ahead of time. He won't lose any pay.'

Nilson shrugged, clearly at a loss as to what was going on, but he left to do as Matt asked.

Once the man was out of earshot, Stevie leaned against the rail and faced him. 'Well?'

'Well, what?'

'You didn't stay in the bedroom last night. Then I find out Tiago has gotten off the boat without a word. I didn't even have a chance to say goodbye to him. Now we're suddenly on our way back…' Her eyes widened. 'That's it, isn't it? You're running away. Because of what went on between us.'

'I told you we needed supplies.' He took a step closer. 'That includes condoms. Has it even dawned on you what could have happened? If you had made the merest suggestion that we…' He jabbed at the air with his index finger, unable to use the strong word that came to mind. 'If you'd climbed on top of me, I wouldn't have stopped you.'

'But I didn't.' She smiled. 'You didn't seem to mind what I did instead.'

He gave her no answering smile. 'That's not the point. I can't trust myself around you.'

'That's funny, because I distinctly remember you asking me if I trusted you. I did.' Her brows went up. 'I still do.'

He gave a harsh laugh. 'Haven't you heard? A man will say anything when it comes to sex.'

'Some might. But you didn't. You kept your word.' She reached up and touched his ear. 'The man who did this to save a pregnant woman's life doesn't say things he doesn't mean. That man keeps his word, no matter what he has to sacrifice.'

He shook his head. 'I'm not that noble, Stevie.' His hand sifted through the loose locks of her hair before tangling his fingers in them and holding her in place. 'I wanted you last night, and I took what I wanted.'

'I wanted it too, Matt. You make it sound ugly, like I had no choice in the matter.'

'It shouldn't have happened.'

'Maybe. But it did.' Her lids lowered until he couldn't read her thoughts. 'It happened, and I liked it. I seem to remember you asking me to say those very words.'

His chest contracted. How could he not remember? Every second was etched in his mind forever. He'd never wipe the memory away no matter how hard he tried.

Which begged the question. Why make her leave if it made no difference in the end?

'I remember.' He smiled, conceding his heart had already made the decision, even if his mind refused to admit it. 'But we still need condoms. Just in case there's a next time.'

Stevie blinked, then laughed, the sound a rainbow mixture of sunshine and rain. 'That's really why we're tearing back to *Coari* like a bat out of hell, isn't it?'

'I already told you, we're out of health kits.'

'Right. Health kits. With a side order of condoms.' She sidled up to him and wrapped her arms around his neck. 'I was afraid you'd decided to get rid of me.'

A wave of guilt rushed over him, but he ignored it, focusing on the soft press of curves against his body. 'Did you?'

There, not really a negation of her question. Not quite a lie.

'I did.' She sighed and nuzzled his neck. 'I'm glad I was wrong.'

He allowed himself one quick kiss before taking a step back, physically and emotionally. 'I think it's better if we don't shake our fists at fate just yet. Not until after we've reached the city and solved at least one problem.'

'You're the boss.' She blinked. 'But I do want to stop in and see Belini. Just for a minute or two. Deal?'

'Deal.'

'Thank you.' Her palm slid over the top of his hand, her pinky catching his and holding on. 'Are you positive you don't want to come back to bed for a while?'

The sensual promise in her voice made all kinds of interesting possibilities kick to life in his skull. But he'd lectured himself on this very thing a half hour ago. Better to wait until his head caught up to his heart before wading past the shallow end of this particular pool.

'Not a good idea under the circumstances.'

She grinned and released him. 'Okay. But don't say I didn't offer.'

The sassy swing of her hips as she headed off in the direction of the bedroom made him have second thoughts.

But who knew what the next few days might bring? The decision of whether to keep Stevie on or not might already be out of his hands. She'd overheard him ask Tracy to find someone else. It would be easy to shrug his shoulders and pretend he'd had no choice in the matter.

Wouldn't it?

No. But sometimes it was better to leave life-and-death decisions to someone else. Matt had found that out the hard way.

The view as they came around the bend in the river made Stevie's heart soar. Her lips curved as she spied several children playing while their mothers washed clothes nearby. Three fishing canoes bobbed against the slow-moving current, the men busy gathering food for the day.

Normal, mundane activities. And compared with what they'd found the first time she'd set foot in this village, it was nothing short of a miracle.

She turned to Matt, who stood nearby. 'They look good. Healthy.'

'They do. But remember we're only staying for an hour or two.'

'Thank you. I just needed to check, you know?'

'I know.' The warm smile he sent her put the final touch on a perfect day. Stevie couldn't have asked for a happier ending to what might have been a tragic tale. She scoured the shoreline. 'I don't see Belini yet.'

'She has a new baby to tend to. If something was wrong, we'd know it by now.'

They passed by one of the fishing boats, and Matt called out greetings. The man aboard nodded back, but he was busy hauling in his net. Small fish flipped and tussled as the water quickly drained through tiny holes, until there was no liquid left.

Stevie looked closer, admiring the fine, tight weave. Strange, most fishing nets had larger holes, didn't they?

'Hell.' The muttered word from beside her made her glance at Matt's face. His jaw was tight as he watched the villager dump the entire load of fish into his boat.

The next canoe in the group did the same, the net featuring an identical narrow weave. It looked so familiar.

She realized why and gasped in shock and dismay. 'They're using the mosquito nets we brought.'

'So I see.'

'But th-they can't. They need those so they don't have another outbreak.'

So much for her perfect day. She sucked down an exasperated breath, then realized she was probably overreacting. It was only two nets after all. The third boat was still using the standard fishing nets, from what she could see in the distance.

Just let it go, Stevie. It's no big loss.

Nilson came on deck and helped them set anchor, before lowering the dinghy in the water. Stevie's excitement returned when she realized how much they had to be thankful for. The fact that the men were fishing was a good sign. It meant everything was okay in the village. At least for now.

Matt leaped into the small boat and then helped Stevie get in. Sitting down, he rowed with strong strokes that emphasized his powerful tanned biceps—a fact that Stevie swore she only noticed in passing—and soon had them on shore.

Leaving Matt so he could locate the chief and announce their arrival, she hurried toward Belini's hut, only to find it empty. Not even the mosquito netting they'd hung was in evidence. Surely she hadn't… A momentary wave of panic hit her before she wrestled it back down.

You're being ridiculous. It's a good sign, not a bad one.

Belini was well enough to leave her house, something she hadn't been able to do the last time she'd seen her. Stevie stepped outside the dwelling and, after stopping to receive several excited greetings from some of the other women, asked if anyone knew where Belini was.

'Perto do rio,' one of them answered.

Strange, Stevie had just come from the river. Had she missed seeing Belini somehow?

She glanced around and spotted Matt in front of the chief's hut and decided she'd better pay her respects as well.

'You are well?' the man asked.

'Yes, very. And you?'

'The village is again healthy.'

Stevie nodded. 'I'm so glad.'

'Your husband is making you happy?'

A sudden rush of heat poured into her face. She'd almost forgotten these people thought she was married to Matt. But this was one question she could answer without lying, because she had been happy for the last couple of days. 'Yes.'

Matt stepped over to her side. 'She wouldn't let me pass Tupari without stopping in to see how the tribe was doing.'

'I went to Belini's hut, but she wasn't there.'

'She's washing vegetables by the river.' The fierce pride on his face was unmistakable.

Matt took her arm. 'I'll help you find her.' He nodded to the chief. 'I'm sorry we can't stay for tonight's ceremony.'

'Next trip,' the man said.

'Of course.'

As they strolled back toward the river, she inhaled deeply allowing the fragrant clean air to rinse her cares away. If paradise existed, this had to be it. 'What ceremony are we missing?'

'Another wedding. I didn't think you were up for a repeat of the last one.' He grinned down at her and fingered his earring. 'I don't know about you, but I haven't fully recovered from ours yet.'

Stevie laughed. 'You're just afraid of getting high from that pipe again.'

'Oh, so it's only me who had trouble, is it? I seem to remember a certain flower that—'

'Ugh. Don't remind me. Let's just find Belini before we're roped into staying the night.'

They reached the river just as the woman in question came out of a stand of trees, the baby wrapped in cloths and strapped to her chest. As soon as she saw them, she dropped the bundle of vegetables she was carrying and ran to Stevie, gripping her in a hug so tight Stevie feared for the baby's well-being.

'You came to visit! I knew you would!'

Stevie slanted Matt a triumphant I-told-you-it-was-the-right-thing-to-do glance as she pulled away from the embrace. 'How's the baby?' She bent closer to see the child. Wide-set eyes, retaining the typical blue cast of all newborns, seemed to stare back at her. 'He's so beautiful.'

'His name is Stevie.'

She straightened quickly and stared into the face of her newfound friend. 'What?'

'You and Mr. Matt save his life. My son will keep a part of you for always.'

Matt squeezed her arm. 'It's a big honor. I've never heard of them using a foreign name for a child.' He'd spoken in English so no one could understand except her.

Unable to stop herself, she leaned forward and kissed Belini's cheek. 'Thank you.'

The other woman ducked her head and placed a hand on her infant's dark, satiny head. 'I pray his path will be similar to yours. That he will be strong and help others. That he will find a suitable mate…just as you have.'

Stevie bit her lip, the lie she and Matt were perpetrating pressing in on her. 'If he has even half of his mother's qualities, he'll be a wonderful person.'

Bending to pick up a white mesh bag filled with green vegetables, Belini smiled. 'Will you stay for the evening's celebration?'

'I'm sorry. We can't. We have to get to Coari.' Now that she knew the people in the village were well, she was as anxious as Matt to reach the city—and to buy those 'special supplies' he'd mentioned.

Belini knelt beside the water and dunked the satchel, allowing the water to fill the bag then lifting it to let the liquid filter through the small holes.

Small holes. White netting.

Recognition swept through her, and her heart sank. 'What are you doing?'

Belini glanced up at her. 'Doing?'

'Is that the mosquito netting from your hut?'

The woman smiled. 'Yes! It is perfect for washing vegetables, is it not?'

'No, it's supposed to be—'

A hand on her arm stopped the rest of her exclamation in mid-sentence. Matt gave a silent shake of his head.

They said their goodbyes while Stevie's anger grew. Everywhere she looked, mosquito nets were being repurposed for other tasks: hanging sacks used to drain the liquid from home-made cheeses and yogurts; small squares used to scrub the bottoms and sides of cooking pots… And she'd even seen one being used as a hair ornament, of all things.

As soon as they boarded the *Projeto Vida,* she turned all that pent-up frustration on Matt. 'How could you stand there and watch them use those nets for other things without saying a word? Without letting me try to explain why they should keep them hung over their beds?' She wanted to scream in fury that all their attempts to help had been for naught. No one in the village felt the slightest hint of guilt. Not even Belini, who'd rambled on and on about how perfect those vital nets were for straining vegetables.

Vegetables! Not a single word about how they'd possibly saved lives in that village.

God, it was like she was reliving her job in New York all over again. She'd tried to talk her ex-fiancé into making policy changes at the hospital that would improve their ability to treat poorer patients. She'd been hobbled at every turn. And when she'd dared to bypass the system and save a life, she'd been shot down—her career stalled and possibly in ruins as a result. So here she was in Brazil, trying to do what she couldn't in New York.

But at least there she'd been allowed to speak her mind.

Matt hadn't given her the chance to say anything back at the village. Not once.

'Those nets could have prevented an epidemic like the one we just witnessed.' She stalked forward, balling her fists and planting them in the center of Matt's chest, only to have him seize her wrists and hold her in place. In the back of her mind she was aware of Nilson quietly vacating the room, probably horrified at her outburst. But she didn't care. If she was going to stay here, she was damn well going to express how she felt about this particular subject.

'Calm down.' The order was soft, but there was a line of steel underlining the words.

'Why? So we can get a call in six months saying there's been an outbreak of yellow fever? That Belini and her baby have died?' She tried to jerk away from him, but he held her in place. Her only option was to glare up at him.

'Do you think you're the first person to pass out mosquito nets to these people?'

'No, of course not.'

His grip on her wrists loosened and he rubbed his thumbs over the chafed skin. 'Once the immediate threat is over, there's always some other danger lurking in the background. A famine. A torn fishing net. Some other need that's not being met. Their lives are ruled by the here and now, not by what the future may or may not hold.'

'Why bother trying to help, then, if nothing ever changes? I came here to make a difference, not to have my efforts tossed in the wind.'

Was she talking about Brazil or her work in New York? Maybe they were one and the same.

'We do what we can to educate them. That doesn't include changing their culture or turning them into 'us.' We have to let them make their own decisions.'

She sagged against him, suddenly exhausted from the barrage of emotions she'd fought all day. 'And if they never make the right ones?'

'Then we've at least given them viable options.'

'You're okay with that? With patching up holes but never treating the root cause?'

'I do treat the cause. I provide them with some of the tools necessary to make changes—just like you did with the netting. It's up to them to use those tools in the way they see fit. We can't force them to do anything.'

Stevie gazed at him. Most of the doctors she'd been around were problem solvers by nature. What kind of man was able to spot the problem, figure out a solution, and then stand by in silence while that solution was ignored?

An extraordinary one.

One she could—Stevie swallowed hard—one she could grow to love with very little encouragement.

The muscles of her throat tightened. One she'd already grown to love.

No! She'd just been engaged to another man a month and a

half ago. A man who'd abused her trust in the worst possible way. There was no way she could have fallen in love with someone else so quickly.

Unless she'd never really loved Michael in the first place. But she'd agreed to marry him—had wanted to be with him. How could she not have loved him?

Rebound.

These slippery, elusive fits of emotion had to be the result of feeling rejected. Unloved.

Even as she thought the words, her heart pitched them to the side. This had nothing to do with her and everything to do with the man whose heart she could hear beating beneath her cheek.

Just as she started to pull away, horrified at the wishy-washiness of her emotions, she spied Nilson in the doorway.

She eased away from Matt, nodding toward the crew member.

'Mateus, Miss Tracy is on the radio. She said she needs to speak with you immediately.'

Stevie's heart leaped to her throat and all kinds of dire predictions swirled around in her head. Another outbreak? Something worse? She could still hear that heated cellphone conversation between Matt and the *Projeto Vida* director right after her arrival. Had Tracy found a replacement for her? Had she decided she didn't want a—what had Matt called it?— 'washed-up doc' sullying her organization's reputation?

No. Surely Matt was the one who made those kinds of decisions, and over the last day or two he hadn't seemed nearly as anxious to be rid of her as he had been.

Her mouth twisted. Yeah, why would he be when she was willing to sprawl flat on her back at the first crooked smile he threw her way?

He wasn't like that. He'd tried to resist what happened as much as she had. And he certainly could have taken it to the next step and then washed his hands of any responsibility.

Instead, they were on their way to buy condoms.

When he tensed and released her hands, she backed up a couple of steps.

'I need to get this,' he said.

'Do you want me to go with you?'

He shook his head, jaw tight. 'No. Tracy and I have a couple of things we need to discuss.'

In private.

He hadn't said the words, but the inference came through loud and clear.

All her doubts and fears leapt back in place, howling and screeching for her to do something.

But there was nothing she could do but nod and let him walk away.

As soon as he went through the door, Nilson came over and laid a hand on her shoulder. 'Your face shows much worry. Why?'

She shook her head. What could she say that would convey she was fine without lying?

Nothing. Because she wasn't fine.

Not by a long shot.

CHAPTER SEVENTEEN

'STILL ticked at me?' The connection was clear enough this time that the trace of chagrin behind Tracy's words came through loud and clear.

'I was ready to wring your neck a couple of weeks ago.'

'Not any more?' Leave it to Tracy to pick up on the real meaning behind his words. Besides, she was right. He was well over his anger.

When had that happened? His mind flashed through various scenes and came up with Stevie as she'd looked at their wedding celebration—her kohl-darkened eyes giving her a wild and untamed appearance. The way she'd gripped his hand so tightly as the medicine man had pierced his ear.

'No, I'm not furious any more. In fact, I've decided to keep Stevie on the team, so you can stop looking.'

An awkward pause ensued. 'That could be a bit of a problem. I'm leaving for Coari tonight. When can you be back?'

He frowned, her words making him uneasy. 'We're actually headed there now. We should dock some time tomorrow afternoon. Why?'

'Well…' She drew the word out like an omen. 'You were so upset at me for hiring a woman that I made a few phone calls.'

'And?' Why had he insisted on Tracy finding someone else before he'd even given Stevie a fair chance?

'A doctor in London has expressed an interest in the position, and I also called Craig. We had a surprisingly productive chat. He's willing to give *Projeto Vida* another shot.'

'Craig? The guy practically had to be medevac'd out of Brazil.' What was Tracy thinking?

'Yes, well, he thinks he might have been too hasty.'

Tracy hadn't seen the look on the man's face when he'd said, 'I'm done.'

There was more to this than met the ear. 'What'd you promise him? I know he's not just offering just because he missed me.'

She laughed. 'You caught me. I promised him a month off every year.' A beat went by. 'With pay.'

'You're kidding, right?' Tracy was a female version of Scrooge. She took pride in squeezing every dollar until it begged for mercy. He couldn't imagine her giving away a month's salary.

'I couldn't get the London guy to agree right away. I started to panic. I know you, Matt. You'll eventually run Stevie off and then work yourself to death just to prove some kind of twisted point. You need another doctor on that team. You know it, and I know it.'

'There's already someone here—who I haven't run off, by the way—so let's just leave things the way they are.'

Something that was either a snort or a burst of static came through the speaker. 'Let's just leave it? I thought you were going to have an aneurism when you learned Stevie was a woman.'

'And you had no hand in that little deception, right?' He couldn't keep the dryness out of his voice.

'I know how you play when you're all by yourself. It's not pretty.' Tracy gave a quick laugh. 'I had no choice but to hire her. And as far as you suddenly wanting her to stay, I find that hard to believe. You were pretty emphatic about replacing her the last time I talked to you.'

He fiddled with his earring, wondering if he had enough time to take the thing out and let the piercing heal so Tracy didn't catch a glimpse of it. Except Matt didn't want to take it out.

How ridiculous was that? He'd allowed Stevie to think he was keeping the bead in because of the village, but that wasn't the only reason. Not by a long shot.

He decided a noncommittal answer was the way to go. 'She's working out better than I expected. What can I say?'

Silence.

'Trace? You still there?'

'I'm here. I kind of promised Craig I'd bring him back on board. Besides, there's another slight prob—'

'Well, *un*-promise him.'

She sighed. 'I'm not sure that's wise. Listen, I'll be there in the morning. We can discuss it then.'

'Why not do it now, over the radio? Or by e-mail…I'll have access once we reach the city. There's no real reason for you to come up here.' Especially when he hadn't sorted out everything in his head.

'This is something that should be done in person.'

A chill went over him. 'Are you firing me?'

'Of course not! What on earth is wrong with you, Matt?'

He ran a hand over his neck, the pain that had receded over the last week returning as his muscles tensed. 'Nothing. We probably won't be back in time to pick you up from the airport.'

'That's okay. I'll hire a car and meet you at the boat. Same docking site, right?'

'Right.'

As soon as he signed off, he headed back up to the deck, where he stared out at the water. He caught his reflection in one of the few pieces of chrome still attached to the boat. A flash of something caught his eye and he leaned closer.

The polished bead in his ear. Wouldn't Tracy love that? He could hear the questions already.

Questions for which he had no answer.

Take it out before she sees it.

Even as he fingered the bead, ordering himself to untie the knot holding it place, he stood there like an impotent fool.

What was wrong with him?

You'd think he was taking off his wedding band. He glanced down at his empty ring finger. It had taken him losing the ring in the river to get him to finally acknowledge his wife wasn't coming back. He'd searched the water for hours afterwards, but had realized that it was gone. Forever.

Just like Vickie.

To take the earring out of his ear would be like losing Stevie, too, and he wasn't ready to do that.

Not yet.

Maybe not ever.

Damn Tracy for coming to see him. Now of all times.

He had this niggling pain in his gut and knew exactly what it meant: he was in trouble. Big trouble.

As much as he told himself that Tracy calling Craig was his own doing, and probably for the best, he just felt like giving someone a pounding.

And that someone was him.

She couldn't see Coari. Not yet. Matt had told her they'd be there within the hour, and that Tracy would meet them at the dock. At this point the longer it took to arrive, the better.

Despite her best efforts, worry had chewed several holes through her insides. First Matt had said they were rushing back because he wanted to buy supplies. Supplies that included condoms. The implication was that they'd be making love again. Then he'd returned from having a private conversation with Tracy, and the anticipation that had been building between them fizzled. Whatever he'd discussed with his supervisor had him worried.

His easy smile had disappeared. As had the intimate little touches she'd come to cherish.

As soon as breakfast was over the next day, he'd dismantled all evidence of his sleeping arrangements, claiming it was normal preparation for docking. Nilson, however, wasn't tearing around his quarters, getting ready to disembark. Neither did Matt ask her to take down her hammock.

She sighed. But at least he hadn't asked her to pack her bags. So she'd stubbornly left everything in her room. Until she was told otherwise, she planned to continue her work.

The boat motored around a bend, and there it was. Coari.

From this distance, the reddish-beige buildings seemed orchestrated to match the muddy color of the river. If not for the small strip of green along the water's edge, she'd swear the water had reached up and kissed the small city, leaving its own indelible mark.

This was the place she'd first set eyes on the *Projeto Vida*. The SUV Matt had used to pick her up from the airport was still parked in the same spot, a powdery layer of dust now coating the surface. It seemed like a lifetime ago she'd sat inside the vehicle, staring in dismay at the decrepit medical vessel.

The freshly glossed finish on the deck winked up at her, and she half smiled. Even without that minor improvement, she now saw the boat with new eyes.

As they drew closer, she noticed a woman stood at the dock, waving. Even from this distance, Stevie could tell she was beautiful. Long dark hair hung just below her shoulders with a fringe of bangs framing a delicate face. Where her own body was lean, almost tomboyish, this woman was the epitome of a pin-up girl. Voluptuous. Curvy.

A bombshell.

No man in his right mind could help but notice her.

A twinge of something ugly whisked up her spine. Maybe Matt preferred women that were soft and lush.

She mashed the jealousy back down. That was ridiculous. When Matt stood beside her, giving the woman on the dock a half-wave of acknowledgement, Stevie tried to summon up some enthusiasm. Unfortunately, she found very little to work with.

'Are you ready for this?' His voice, still full of tension, warned her something was very wrong.

'I'm not sure. Are you?' She glanced up at him, her eyes instinctively seeking the bead in his left ear. There it was, still on display. Relief swept through her along with a strange sense of ownership. Surely he knew he'd have to explain why he was now sporting an earring.

It would have been easy for him to take it out and hide what had happened between them.

But he hadn't.

'We'll soon find out,' he muttered.

The second they reached the dock, Tracy hurried over to greet them. Matt leaped the short space between the boat and wooden planks and enveloped the woman in a warm hug. Stevie swallowed, grabbing the handrail to ease herself across the gap. Hopefully the boat wouldn't lurch, sending her careening into the water.

Matt released the woman and secured Stevie's elbow, steadying her as she tried to get her land legs back under her.

'I don't think you two have met in person,' he said. 'Tracy Hinton, this is Stevie Wilson.'

Tracy smiled, leaning forward to kiss both her cheeks in the Brazilian fashion. 'I've heard so much about you.'

'You have?' Stevie and Matt spoke at the same time, and she couldn't suppress an answering smile.

Tracy laughed. 'Yes, but the reason for that will come soon enough. Tell me about your trip. Was the dengue outbreak as bad as we feared?'

'Worse.' Matt proceeded to give Tracy a quick rundown on the village, looking at Stevie from time to time to fill in the blanks. She noticed he made no mention of the wedding ceremony.

As if the other woman read her thoughts, she raised her brows. 'Aren't you leaving out one crucial detail?'

Dull color crept up Matt's neck. 'Not sure what you mean.'

'Your ear, silly.' Tracy reached up and fingered the new addition, moving closer to study the bead. 'How did this come about?'

Something about the easy intimacy between the two of them set off warning bells in her head.

Matt seemed to hesitate. 'It's just—'

'Gratitude,' Stevie interrupted him, turning to give him a fake smile. 'Don't be so bashful.'

She turned to Tracy. 'Matt saved the chief's daughter, and the village was so grateful they marked him as one of their own during a special ceremony.'

Okay, it wasn't the entire truth, but she suddenly didn't want this woman to know what she and Matt had been through…what they'd done. She didn't want Tracy knowing about the *ayahuasca* pipe or the magical flowers.

Or about the night they'd shared.

She had no idea what Matt and Tracy were to each other, and the thought of being cast the part of naïve fool—yet again—made her cringe. For all she knew, these two could be lovers.

Tracy tilted her head and studied Stevie. 'Wow. Matt's been working this river for twelve years. It's about damn time he had something to show for it.'

His eyes met Stevie's, and something sizzled just below the surface. 'You're right. It's about damn time.'

Her palms tingled, and she pressed them against her slacks to dull the sensation. Was he talking about the villagers, or about her…and him?

'Well,' said Tracy, breaking the sudden silence, 'I have a couple of rooms reserved at the *pousada*.' She smiled at Stevie. 'And I have a surprise for you.'

'For me?'

Tracy nodded, only to have Matt speak up. 'If it's regarding what we discussed on the radio, I need to speak with you privately about that.'

'That's fine.' She strolled toward a grey Land Rover. 'Let's wait until we reach the *pousada*, okay?'

Stevie was relegated to the back seat, while Tracy and Matt sat up front and discussed *Projeto Vida* business. She had no idea what surprise Tracy had in store for her, but unless it included a deep tub and a jar of scented salts she didn't much care. Even a normal shower with plenty of hot, clean water would be enough to satisfy her at the moment. Leaning her head against the headrest, she allowed her eyes to close. Exhaustion crept over her bit by bit, until the road bumps melded together into a constant drone that lulled her toward the edge of consciousness.

'Stevie, honey, wake up.' Her eyes flickered open, and she caught Matt sliding onto the seat next to her. He smiled and brushed his fingers across her cheek.

Where was Tracy? The front seat of the car was empty.

Wait…had he just called her 'honey'?

She shook her head, trying to clear it. 'Are we here?'

'Yep. Tracy's gone in to get the room keys.' He glanced toward a simple white building on the right-hand side of the car. 'Once we're settled, I'd like to go for a walk. Just the two of us. I have something I need to tell you.'

Was this it? The big let-down?

Stevie bit her lip. 'Is it about Tracy?'

'Tracy?' He frowned. 'No. It's about us.'

'About us? So you and Tracy aren't…?'

'Aren't…?' His brows went up. 'Good God, no. She's my sister-in-law. Vickie's younger sister.'

Shock rolled through her. 'I had no idea.'

He eased out of the car, taking her hand to help her out as well. 'There's no way you could have. I didn't expect you to be here long enough for it to matter.' He sighed. 'There's a lot we need to talk about, but it can wait. We have plenty of time. That is, if you're serious about sticking around. If not, now's the time to speak up.'

Hope began to build in her chest. It sounded like he *wanted* her to stay. 'Yes. Of course I'm serious.'

They went into the hotel and found Tracy on the phone. She smiled at them and passed two sets of keys to Matt.

He grabbed a pad and scribbled something then shoved it towards Tracy. She scanned it, then gave him a thumbs-up sign before turning back to her call.

'Where are we going?' Stevie asked as Matt pushed through the door, towing her behind him.

'Where do you want to go?'

'I noticed Tracy rented separate rooms for us.' She hesitated. 'Would you think me forward if I said I wanted to go back to yours?'

'No, because I was thinking the very same thing.' He smiled down at her, his blue eyes darkening. 'But, for both our sakes, we need to make a side trip first.'

* * *

They came out of the drug store with a tiny bag, the pink tint to Stevie's cheeks doing a number on his heart.

'Are you sure you're okay with this?' he asked.

'Definitely. It was my idea, remember?'

He gripped her hand as they rounded the corner, heading back toward his hotel room.

'How are we going to explain to Tracy why we're not joining…?' Her voice faded away, and when he glanced down, he saw her eyes had gone wide, the green irises turning a stormy grey.

She released his hand, and at first he thought it was because Tracy stood on the patio of the hotel. Then he noticed she was deep in conversation with a tall man in a business suit. Stevie stopped in her tracks just as Tracy and her companion turned toward them.

Strangely, when the man gave them a brilliant smile and strode toward them, Stevie stumbled back a step or two, a couple of garbled sounds erupting from her throat.

Before he had a chance to ask her what was wrong, the man reached them. He bypassed Matt altogether, stopping in front of Stevie. When he bent and dropped a kiss on her open mouth, anger roiled through Matt's system. His hands fisted and he started to move forward, but Tracy appeared at his side, her fingers gripping his forearm and holding him in place.

'I told you I had a surprise for her.' She kept her voice low. 'He's the CEO from Stevie's hospital. He flew in from New York yesterday.'

CHAPTER EIGHTEEN

CEO? Since when did chief executive officers kiss their employees on the mouth?

He shook free of Tracy's restraining hand but remained where he was, not sure what was going on. Had Tracy called Stevie's former boss and asked him to come?

The man leaned back and surveyed Stevie with a raised brow. 'My God…look at you.'

Instead of laughing, like she might have done with Matt, Stevie's hands went to her shirt and straightened it self-consciously. A sliver of apprehension lodged in his gut.

'What are you doing here, Michael? I told you we were through.' She seemed dazed, as if his appearance had been the furthest thing from her mind.

Through? What the hell was she talking about?

'I came to talk some sense into you. I had no idea our little argument would drive you to do something so extreme.' One side of his mouth curled up in a half-smile. 'I can see I'll have to make it up to you for a good long time when we get back.'

A sick sense of dread began pumping through Matt's veins.

'You don't have to make anything up to me. I'm not going back.'

'Of course you are. I mean, look at this place. It looks just as bad in person as it did in the medical journal's help-wanted ad.' He chucked her under the chin, ignoring the fact that she ducked away from his hand. 'Doctors Without Borders it is not.

We sat in bed and laughed over the pictures of this…operation, remember?'

The words 'bed' and 'laughed' grabbed Matt by the throat.

Stevie's eyes darted toward him, brimming with guilt. 'No, I…'

It was true.

She *had* laughed—had thought *Projeto Vida* was ridiculous. And this man had been in bed with her.

The CEO of her hospital.

Jealousy and hurt swirled around inside Matt, each seeking to outrank the other.

As if realizing he'd made some kind of faux pas with his last comment, the man glanced their way and made a half-hearted attempt to backpedal. 'No offense. I'm sure it's for a great cause.' Even as he said it, he pulled a spotless white handkerchief from the inner pocket of his jacket and brushed at a spot of dust on the leg of his expensive trousers. The square of cloth disappeared back inside his coat.

'I don't want you here, Michael. How did you even find me?'

'Your doorman. Thank God you held onto your lease, you're going to need it. I had no idea you'd be willing to chuck your whole career on a whim.'

She laughed, the sound hard and brittle. 'A whim? Hardly. You made sure of that with the board of directors.'

'I overreacted. I met with the board a week ago, and they realize—like I do—that you were merely concerned about your patient. They want you back. *I* want you back. You're too valuable a doctor to waste your talent in a place like this.' He touched her hand. 'Just so you know, I didn't cancel our honeymoon reservations.'

Honeymoon? This guy was her fiancé?

She'd mentioned being involved with someone, but she'd said it was over. The words 'engaged' and 'fiancé' had never come up in the conversation.

A sinking sensation spiraled through him, and his fingers tightened around the sack containing the new package of condoms—and what he'd thought was a new beginning. He glanced at Tracy and read the pity in her eyes.

She knew.

'You were engaged?' he asked Stevie. 'Why didn't you tell me?'

She'd let him do things to her. Intimate things. And what she'd done to him… He closed his eyes, trying to block that particular memory.

'It was complicated,' she said. 'But you're right. I should have.'

Complicated.

The woman knew personal details about his life. About his marriage. And he suddenly realized how little she'd told him about her past.

The other man's eyes narrowed, maybe sensing there was more here than he realized. 'Stevie and I had a slight disagreement. Most couples do at some point.'

'Maria was more than a disagreement, don't you think, Michael?'

A tightening of lips from the other man was the only sign that her words had hit a nerve. 'I made a mistake. That's something we can discuss later. In private.' There was a definite emphasis on the last two words.

'There's nothing to discuss.'

Tracy, clearly uncomfortable with the ugly turn this little reunion had taken, glanced at Matt and tilted her head, indicating they should move away. He was having none of it.

Instead, he took a step toward the couple, noting the way Michael edged slightly in front of Stevie, blocking Matt's access.

'Is this why you came to Brazil?' he asked her. 'Because you had a falling out with your hospital and your fiancé?'

'No.'

'Yes.'

She and Michael spoke at the same time, but their answers were poles apart.

'Which is it, Stevie?'

'I ran into some trouble with the board at my hospital, but

that's not the only reason I came here. I'd been thinking about it for a while.'

Her ex fiancé let out a laugh of disbelief. 'Is that so? We've been engaged for two years and you never once mentioned coming to Brazil.' He turned to Matt. 'I'll tell you why she came. Her hospital privileges were suspended for refusing to follow hospital protocol.'

'Michael, please don't do this.'

Matt swallowed. She'd lied. About everything. She'd said she came to Brazil to 'make a difference'. The truth was, she'd been tossed out of her old job and had needed another one pronto. *Projeto Vida*'s desperation in that series of ads must have come through loud and clear.

The ads she and Mr. Smooth CEO had laughed their heads off at. *Projeto Vida* was Matt's lifeblood, and she'd ridiculed it.

A wave of nausea almost brought him to his knees.

Another thought hit. This man was the CEO of the hospital where she worked, and she'd slept with him.

The condom package whispered an accusation. She'd slept with one boss—what was to keep her from sleeping with another? She'd been worried about him sending her back to the States. Could she have led him on? Reeled him in with those big innocent eyes and that sexy accent?

What had she said?

I thought for sure I'd...persuaded you to keep me on. He swallowed. She had persuaded him. He'd been this close to telling her that he...

The solution came to him in an instant.

He turned to Michael. 'Your timing worked out perfectly. Tracy has someone who's interested in Stevie's position.' His glance clipped Stevie's, but he found he couldn't quite meet her eyes. 'You knew we were looking for someone else. The boat just isn't built to house both male and female doctors. And you saw what happened with Belini's tribe.'

Stevie's lips parted. 'Oh, but you said—'

'I know what I said.' And he'd been wrong, on so many counts. But he was about to undo all those mistakes in one cruel cut. 'The doctor who was here before you has decided to come back. We gave him that option, and feel it's only right we keep our word.'

'What? When did this happen?'

'Tracy told me about it on the radio yesterday.'

'Yesterday. And yet today you were willing to let me…' She motioned to the sack he held and a soft glitter of tears washed into her eyes. 'Oh, God.'

He almost cracked. Almost told her it was all a misunderstanding. But as she wiped a trickle of moisture from her left cheek, Michael put his arm around her and pulled her close.

Matt's resolve stiffened. How long before she decided Brazil wasn't for her? A month? A year? She'd eventually miss the career she'd had in New York, he was sure of it.

Better to allow her think he was a bastard and get it over with than watch her walk away later, trampling his heart beneath her feet. 'Can you manage your things, or would you like Nilson's help?'

A long silence ensued. Part of him hoped she'd argue with him…tell him she wasn't going anywhere. Instead, her chin went up, and she met his gaze, her face a study in angry defiance. 'Don't worry, I'll have my stuff off the boat within the hour.'

'I appreciate it. Let Tracy know if you need help booking a flight out.' With that he turned on his heel and headed in the direction of the hotel bar. He needed a drink. The stronger, the better. As he reached the door, something made him stop and glance back. Her eyes were still following him. Needing to make his point perfectly clear, he raised his brows and tossed the bag from the drugstore—along with all his hopes—into a nearby trashcan. She'd get his meaning.

They were through.

He didn't need her.

He didn't need anyone.

Matt endured the playful punch to his arm with gritted teeth and a sour stomach.

'Admit it. You couldn't live without me.' If Craig only knew how close he was to having that grin wiped off his face, he'd

stop his incessant quest for praise. 'I did a beautiful job sutur-
ing that little native girl's arm, didn't I? The scar will hardly be
noticeable.'

Little native girl? Of all the condescending, ignorant…

Tiago, fresh from his forced two-week hiatus, stepped ner-
vously between the pair. *'Calma, Mateus.'*

Calm down? He was perfectly calm. He glanced down at his
balled fists and frowned. Uncurling them, he forced the tense
muscles to relax. His hands weren't the only body part feeling
the strain. His neck had been killing him for the past few days.
What he wouldn't give to have Stevie's magic hands smooth
away his pain.

She's gone. It's what you said you wanted, remember?

He forced his mind back to Tiago. 'How's Nilson?'

'He's on the deck, fishing for our lunch. But he said you will
not keep him from the real work much longer. He claims you are
stealing his manhood by giving him jobs fit for an infant.'

While Matt had agonized over that mosquito bite on Stevie's
arm, no one had had any idea that Nilson had also been exposed
to dengue. And in the end it had been his crewmember who'd
fallen ill. With Tiago still at his home village, and Stevie's abrupt
departure, it had been Matt who'd nursed Nilson during the long
nights when the fever had caused tremors so strong, two of the
man's teeth had broken. It was Matt who'd strapped Nilson's arm
to the metal railing of the examination table to hold it still while
he'd inserted tubing for the saline drip. Yet even while Nilson
had quaked and moaned in pain, he'd insisted he wanted to work,
his pride fierce even while he'd lain weak and helpless.

Something about the experience had brought Stevie to mind.
What if she'd been the one…

Matt shook his head to clear it. 'Nilson still needs a few more
days to recoup his strength. Tell him he's too valuable for me to
lose.'

Even as he said it, he noticed Craig studying the inner surface
of his arms yet again, rubbing at something, his teasing attitude
long gone.

'What are you doing?' Matt asked.

'That man could still be contagious. I can't believe you let him stay on the boat with the rest of us. He should have been quarantined.' He sniffed. 'If I had known he had dengue before I got on that flight, I would have delayed my trip.'

This time it was Tiago whose jaw tightened. The two crew members had been with *Projeto Vida* from its inauguration, twelve years ago. Tiago wasn't going to stand by while Craig whined about exposure as if Nilson were nothing more than a disease vector.

Matt stared the other doctor down. '*That man* has a name. I'll thank you to use it.'

'Of course, I didn't mean anything. It's just that when Tracy called me the second time, she sounded almost desperate, said you'd had another doctor leave unexpectedly.' He shrugged. 'I guess I'm not the only one who had trouble adjusting to life on the Amazon.'

Except Stevie hadn't had trouble adjusting. She'd thrown herself into the job, never balking at the rough conditions, her compassion toward Belini and her baby...toward everyone...had been boundless. She'd cared enough about their well-being to get angry—really angry—when they'd cut up the mosquito nets and used them for other things.

While he'd freaked out over her mosquito bite, she'd been the voice of reason, insisting on finishing what she'd started.

Matt swallowed. And he'd been stupid enough to send her away.

Ah, hell. He'd been an idiot. A fearful, insecure half-wit, scared out of his mind of losing another woman he cared about.

That's why he'd jumped at the chance to get rid of Stevie. And why he'd allowed himself to believe that Brazil had been a last-ditch effort to save her career. It was obvious to everyone that she liked it here. That she'd wanted to stay.

With him.

He hadn't been angry over her reasons for coming to Brazil. Or that she'd recently ended a bad relationship. No, those were only excuses. Lies. The real reason he'd wanted her gone ran deeper. And was much more personal.

Matthew Grant Palermo had been terrified.

Terrified something would strike Stevie down and take her away from him. Terrified that she'd make him fall in love with her, only to abandon him when a better opportunity came along. So he'd thrown her away, taken away her choice to stay…or to leave.

He'd been a selfish bastard.

He loved her, dammit. His fingers went to his ear. It was the reason he still had his earring in place. He was married. In heart, if not in law.

And if he *had* succeeded in driving her back into her former fiancé's arms, he would kick himself to the United States and back again.

But he was going. He had to see her. If she'd still have him.

He clapped Tiago on the back and faced his soon-to-be ex-colleague. 'Craig, it's time for you to sink or swim, because I have somewhere I need to be. You can take over for me while I'm gone. Or you can fly back to the States. Your choice.'

'B-but, you can't just leave me here alone. I just got here.' When Matt said nothing, Craig's horrified expression changed, his brows sweeping down over his nose in a scowl. 'I should have known there was more to this story than Tracy let on. I'm out of here.'

The test had worked like a charm. Matt closed his eyes and sucked down a deep breath, relishing the earthy fragrance that rose off the *Rio Preto*. 'The good news is you've helped me realize what a jerk I've been. But that's about to change.'

'You haven't exactly been a jerk. You just can't leave—'

'You are going to fetch Miss Stevie, then?' Tiago stared at him, hope shining in his eyes.

'I am.'

Craig jammed his hands on his hips. 'Who the hell is Stevie?'

'Stevie Wilson…is going to be your replacement. If I can get her to take me back.' Without a backward glance, he strode away to check on Nilson and to find his passport.

CHAPTER NINETEEN

STEVIE shoved back a strand of hair that had escaped her clip as she made her way to the patient in exam room three. Pulling the file from the holder, she gave it a quick perusal and then pushed through the heavy door.

'Hello, Mary, how's that back of yours holding up?'

She listened to the woman's progress, her eyes going to the small bump on Mary's midsection. Not quite forty, her pregnancy had been as much a surprise as the two compression fractures in her thoracic spine, the latter diagnosis sending her to the clinic where Stevie now worked. Mary was proof that even in developed countries poor early nutrition could have devastating consequences. As did the soft, cushy lives technology afforded.

Belini came to mind. Then Matt. She gritted her teeth and forced her concentration back to the woman in front of her.

'You're not riding that Appaloosa of yours at anything faster than a walk, right?' A seasoned barrel racer and equine trainer, horses were Mary's lifeblood. Her profession. Or they had been. Only time would tell if they could coax enough bone growth to stand up to the wear and tear of future competitions.

Tears came to the woman's eyes. 'It's hard.' She touched her stomach. 'It's one thing to stop riding temporarily, for the sake of the baby. It's another to wonder if this is it. The end of all my hopes and dreams.'

Been there. Done that. Had the emotional scars to prove it.

She laid a hand on the woman's shoulder. 'Let's give your body some time. The fractures have healed, but we still need to get you into physical therapy to strengthen those back muscles.' She smiled. 'Besides, I've been doing some research of my own. I took riding lessons when I was a teenager. Western Pleasure. I even have a ribbon or two under my belt to show for it.'

Mary laughed, her eyes crinkling. 'You actually rode a peanut pusher?'

'A what?'

'It's a nickname. Some Western Pleasure horses are trained to carry their heads so low they look like they're pushing peanuts along the ground.'

'Ah.' Stevie did remember seeing that phrase in her reading. She'd also read that that style of riding was no longer in vogue. 'I think you'd be surprised at how the headset has changed over the years. Don't rule out the possibility just yet. Barrels and Western Pleasure may be poles apart on a thrill scale, but I remember Western Pleasure being a whole lot harder than it looked. And the soft, slow movements are easier on the bones and joints than running Barrels. You'd be learning a whole new discipline. Look on it as a challenge.'

Mary frowned as if she was considering Stevie's words. 'I'd never thought about changing tracks. I'd miss what I did, but I guess it's better than giving up riding all together.'

Stevie could definitely relate. She missed Brazil. But practicing in Atlanta was better than giving up medicine altogether. And at least she didn't have to face her ex-fiancé on a daily basis. Once the disciplinary note had been cleared from her record, she'd applied to a variety of clinics. The one in Atlanta had agreed to take her on a six-month trial basis.

Kind of like Matt and Tracy had done. Except they'd agreed to give her two years. Matt had given her less than a tenth of that.

It was the second time she'd been kicked to the curb at the whim of an angry man. She had no intention of it ever happening again.

Mary glanced down at her watch. 'Whew! You must have other patients, and I need to pick Alex up from school.' She stood and gathered her purse, then gave Stevie a quick hug. 'Thank you. You've actually given me a glimmer of hope. My contesting horse won't be very happy with me, but he'll get over it.'

Once Mary left the room, Stevie plunked down onto the examination stool and took a slow, careful breath. Her chest ached, but it had nothing to do with physical pain. Any time she had a few moments to herself, she thought about Matt. About Nilson and Tiago. About Belini. She worked herself to the point of exhaustion each day, trying to blot out that painful chapter in her life.

But it stuck with her in a way that Michael's betrayal never had. The fact that she'd gotten over her ex so quickly should have warned her the relationship had been doomed from the outset. She'd hoped the same would happen with her feelings for Matt. That they'd fade away as she immersed herself in her new job.

They hadn't.

But it was either go on with her life or curl up in a corner somewhere. She wasn't made that way. Like Mary, when faced with difficult circumstances, she would change and adapt. Create new and more realistic expectations.

Penny, one of the nurses, stuck her head around the door. 'You have a patient in exam room two.'

Stevie frowned. 'I thought Mary was the last patient of the day.'

'She was, but someone called in a favor from Dr. Henry. Supposedly an emergency case.'

'Supposedly?'

'You let me know once you've examined him.' Penny snorted and thrust a file into her hand. 'Have fun. The guy refuses to put on a gown.'

'Just my luck. Do you mind sticking around for a few more minutes?'

'Are you kidding? I wouldn't miss this for the world.'

Stevie flipped open the chart, puzzled at the large swath of blank space. It wasn't like Penny not to be thorough. 'There's nothing on here. What's he complaining of?'

'He says he has a crick in his neck, and you've been the only doctor who could make it go away.'

'Me? He must be thinking of someone else. I've haven't treated anyone's neck since medical...'

Stevie's thoughts blanked out as memories crowded in. It couldn't be. She dropped the file on the exam table, her hands suddenly shaking.

'Dr. Wilson, are you all right?'

'I don't know.' She hurried down the hall and stopped outside exam room two. Her hands touched the door, then retracted. She forced down a couple of deep breaths.

Get a grip, Stevie. It's not him. It can't be.

Her heart didn't believe her. This time, when she reached for the door, she forced herself to push through it, readying herself for the wave of disappointment that would surely follow. She stopped in her tracks when she saw a familiar sweep of dark hair.

Propped against a wall, Matt was thumbing through the latest edition of the *Journal of the American Medical Association*. For a second, she wondered if she was having some kind of awful hallucination. She'd thought about Matt almost constantly since coming back to the States. She dreamed about him at night. Had her mind somehow conjured him up from nothing?

Then his blue eyes met hers, and she knew he was no hallucination. He was real. Here in Atlanta.

'How did you find me?' The croaked words were the best she could manage, considering the thick layer of sawdust now clogging her throat.

'Michael.'

She blinked. 'Michael?'

'Your ex seemed to take issue with you leaving his hospital. A few sympathetic clucks from me, and he spilled everything.'

It figured. 'Not very professional of either of you.'

He dropped the magazine on the counter. 'I've done several unprofessional things since meeting you. I came to apologize.'

Crossing her arms over her chest, she tried to appear braver than she felt. If he'd come out of some misplaced sense of guilt for how he'd dumped her, he could take his remorse and fly right back to Brazil.

'No need.' She motioned to the space around her. 'As you can see, I landed on my feet.'

'You didn't go back to Michael. Or to his hospital.'

'Not that it's any of your business but, no. I told you, it was over. Working with him would have been awkward. Besides, I love it here in Atlanta. I can't think of anyplace I'd rather be.'

What was one more lie?

He scrubbed a hand through his hair, and Stevie caught sight of his left ear, where the wedding bead still resided. 'I see. Maybe I've wasted a trip, then.'

Why was he here, anyway? Surely he hadn't traveled four thousand miles just to say he was sorry.

'How's the new guy working out?' The name came to her. 'Craig…wasn't it?'

Matt fiddled with the discarded magazine, his thumb ruffling the pages as he avoided her eyes. 'Yes. And he's not.'

'Really? What happened?'

His gaze came up and speared hers, the electric blue standing out against the sea of tanned skin. 'He wasn't you.'

'He wasn't…' Three small words, but somehow she must have misunderstood them. Or maybe her subconscious had placed the words in his mouth. 'I'm sorry, could you say that again?'

He closed the distance between them. 'I said, he wasn't you.' One of his hands fisted by his side. 'Nilson got sick.' The words came out in a rush.

'Is he all right?'

'He is now. He came down with dengue right after you left.'

'I'm so sorry. You said he's okay, though.' She wasn't quite sure why he was telling her this.

'He is, but I wasn't. It took Nilson falling ill for me to understand why I wanted you gone. It had nothing to do with your engagement or with your reasons for coming to Brazil.'

Her heart twisted inside her. Was that it? He was going to lay some worse transgression at her doorstep? 'I don't understand.'

'Don't you?'

She shook her head, words sticking in her throat.

'When Tracy went to get the keys for our hotel rooms, I asked if you planned on sticking around. Do you remember?'

She remembered every second, right down to the brilliant flare of hope that had erupted inside her belly. An hour later, though, he'd ground out the tiny flame. 'Yes, but I don't see what that has to do with anything.'

Penny peeked in the door. 'Everything all right in here?'

'Fine,' they both said in unison.

'Okay, then…' said the woman, her eyes wide as she let the door click shut.

Matt took one of her hands. 'When I saw Michael standing there…when he kissed you, I realized you might leave, whether I told you to go or not. Or maybe you'd decide to stay, but something else could take you away from me. Something beyond my control.'

She realized what he was getting at. 'Like dengue.'

'Yes. Only I didn't understand that at the time. I only saw a way to relieve the fear that was eating me alive, and I jumped at the chance.'

'Did it help?'

He gave a harsh laugh. 'No. Because by that time it was too late. I was already in love with you.'

'You were in love with me?' She pleaded with herself not to go down this road again, but it was no use. Her heart didn't want to listen to the very rational argument her intellect laid before it.

Because he loved her!

Matt continued, 'So, it's either live with the fear and take a shot at happiness, or live without it and be miserable.'

'And are you? Miserable?'

His hand tightened on hers. 'Every single day without you has been hell. When Tiago found out I was headed for the States, he dove off the boat yelling "Hallelujah".'

Stevie smiled at the image and moved closer, laying her hands on his chest. 'I've been miserable too.'

'Have you?'

'Yes.' She tilted her head back. 'You're not the only one who fell in love on that trip.'

A huge sigh shuddered through his frame, and he dropped a kiss on her lips. 'Thank God,' he whispered against them.

'I want to go back to Brazil.'

'What about your work here?'

'There's a trial period.'

'And if you decide you like it better here?'

She shook her head. 'I won't. Not if you aren't with me.' Reaching up, she smoothed the frown lines from his brow. 'Are you sure you can you do this?'

'Do what?'

'Live with the fear?'

He sighed, threading his fingers through her hair. 'I can't promise not to worry. I'll probably drive you crazy at times.'

'And I can't promise I won't get sick, that I won't die. But I can promise to be careful. As long as you promise to do the same.'

He fingered his earring. 'I've already made the biggest promise I know how to make. But I want to make it official. Will you marry me? Before God and everyone?'

Stevie smiled and pulled him down for a lingering kiss. 'Too late, silly. I already did.'

EPILOGUE

'JU-JU, you come play with me.' The plaintive cry came from Belini's two-year old son, Stevie.

June Christina Palermo, Stevie and Matt's baby girl, stepped toward the other child, her tiny feet unsteady in the sand.

Leaning back against Matt's chest, Stevie sighed. 'It's good to be back, isn't it?'

'I hate to admit it, but yes.' He dropped a kiss on top of her head.

They'd spent almost two years in the States, needing time to nurture their relationship. She'd gotten pregnant and had had June during that time. Stevie had worried the pregnancy would bring back terrible memories of Matt's late wife and unborn child, and it was part of the reason she'd insisted on remaining in the States and having the baby in an Atlanta hospital. She didn't want to put more pressure on Matt than necessary.

The time there had been good—really good—and he'd resisted coming back. But it was time. He'd needed to return to Brazil and see it with an objectivity he'd been lacking. Whether or not they stayed was a decision they'd make together. But hearing the warmth in his voice as he'd greeted the chief, she had a feeling he might not be as against rejoining the *Projeto Vida* team as he'd originally thought.

She tilted her head back and smiled at him. 'Love you.'

'Mmm. I'm glad, because if you didn't...' he nodded toward the children playing in the clearing '...she wouldn't be here right now.'

'I know.' She reached up, feeling for the gold post in his ear, her anniversary present to him last year, before snuggling closer. 'Good thing you came to your senses when you did, or I'd still be working sixty hours a week.'

'Will you miss the practice?'

'Honestly? Yes.' Her eyes swept across the clearing to where the *Rio Preto* flowed past, its current slow and easy. Alive. Free. Carrying life—and death—to the communities that lay along its banks. 'But I miss this too. How about you?'

He chuckled. 'I didn't until we got to the village. But seeing them together...' He tightened his arms around her. 'Yeah, I do.'

'Me too.' She smiled. 'It's perfect isn't it? Our life?'

Belini waved as she walked toward the river's edge, her mosquito-netting sieve filled with vegetables.

Matt gave an audible sigh that seemed to echo her own exasperation. 'No, it's not perfect. But it's close enough.'

Cocking her head for another kiss, she gave him a sassy tilt of her brows. 'That's not what you said last night.'

His mouth captured hers in a searing kiss that made her heart trip a couple of beats and took her back to the slow rock of their hammock as they'd made love in the dark of night. 'Thank heavens Ju-Ju finally caught on to sleeping in her own bed.'

They'd strung a low-lying hammock in the dining area, surrounded by a curtain of mosquito netting. The constant hum of the boat's motor and the way the bed cradled her in its arms did what rocking and cajoling had failed to do for the last two nights, lull their baby into a deep sleep.

'Do we dare hope for two nights in a row?' Stevie asked.

He nodded at Belini. 'I have a better idea. Wait here.'

Walking over to where the other woman knelt, rinsing her vegetables, he whispered something to her. Belini nodded, her eyes shooting to Stevie with a grin.

Matt returned and reached down a hand, which she accepted. But when he tried to lead her toward the village, she hesitated. 'What are you doing?'

'Remember our wedding night?'

Puzzled, she stared at him. 'Of course I do.'

'Not our Stateside wedding. The wedding they threw for us here. In the village.'

Her glance drifted to his ear, a wave of love nearly knocking her over. 'I remember.'

He smiled at her and lifted her fingers to his lips then tugged her along behind him. 'Belini offered to watch Ju-Ju for a couple of hours, and I asked some of the ladies to gather a very special flower and sprinkle its petals around the honeymoon bed.'

'You did?' A strange, shivery sensation passed through her. She lowered her voice. 'Have the men been passing around the pipe again?'

'No. But I wanted things to be perfect this time.'

As they reached the hut and he swept her over the threshold, she saw purple flowers strewn across every available surface. Wrapping her arms around his neck, she breathed in the hypnotic scent that had nothing to do with flowers and everything to do with the man holding her.

Her husband.

For ever.

'Things already are perfect,' she whispered as he leaned in to claim the first of many kisses. 'Because we have each other.'

* * * * *

Mills & Boon® Hardback

January 2012

ROMANCE

The Man Who Risked It All	Michelle Reid
The Sheikh's Undoing	Sharon Kendrick
The End of her Innocence	Sara Craven
The Talk of Hollywood	Carole Mortimer
Secrets of Castillo del Arco	Trish Morey
Hajar's Hidden Legacy	Maisey Yates
Untouched by His Diamonds	Lucy Ellis
The Secret Sinclair	Cathy Williams
First Time Lucky?	Natalie Anderson
Say It With Diamonds	Lucy King
Master of the Outback	Margaret Way
The Reluctant Princess	Raye Morgan
Daring to Date the Boss	Barbara Wallace
Their Miracle Twins	Nikki Logan
Runaway Bride	Barbara Hannay
We'll Always Have Paris	Jessica Hart
Heart Surgeon, Hero...Husband?	Susan Carlisle
Doctor's Guide to Dating in the Jungle	Tina Beckett

HISTORICAL

The Mysterious Lord Marlowe	Anne Herries
Marrying the Royal Marine	Carla Kelly
A Most Unladylike Adventure	Elizabeth Beacon
Seduced by Her Highland Warrior	Michelle Willingham

MEDICAL

The Boss She Can't Resist	Lucy Clark
Dr Langley: Protector or Playboy?	Joanna Neil
Daredevil and Dr Kate	Leah Martyn
Spring Proposal in Swallowbrook	Abigail Gordon

Mills & Boon® Large Print

January 2012

ROMANCE

The Kanellis Scandal	Michelle Reid
Monarch of the Sands	Sharon Kendrick
One Night in the Orient	Robyn Donald
His Poor Little Rich Girl	Melanie Milburne
From Daredevil to Devoted Daddy	Barbara McMahon
Little Cowgirl Needs a Mum	Patricia Thayer
To Wed a Rancher	Myrna Mackenzie
The Secret Princess	Jessica Hart

HISTORICAL

Seduced by the Scoundrel	Louise Allen
Unmasking the Duke's Mistress	Margaret McPhee
To Catch a Husband...	Sarah Mallory
The Highlander's Redemption	Marguerite Kaye

MEDICAL

The Playboy of Harley Street	Anne Fraser
Doctor on the Red Carpet	Anne Fraser
Just One Last Night...	Amy Andrews
Suddenly Single Sophie	Leonie Knight
The Doctor & the Runaway Heiress	Marion Lennox
The Surgeon She Never Forgot	Melanie Milburne

Mills & Boon® Hardback
February 2012

ROMANCE

An Offer She Can't Refuse	Emma Darcy
An Indecent Proposition	Carol Marinelli
A Night of Living Dangerously	Jennie Lucas
A Devilishly Dark Deal	Maggie Cox
Marriage Behind the Façade	Lynn Raye Harris
Forbidden to His Touch	Natasha Tate
Back in the Lion's Den	Elizabeth Power
Running From the Storm	Lee Wilkinson
Innocent 'til Proven Otherwise	Amy Andrews
Dancing with Danger	Fiona Harper
The Cop, the Puppy and Me	Cara Colter
Back in the Soldier's Arms	Soraya Lane
Invitation to the Prince's Palace	Jennie Adams
Miss Prim and the Billionaire	Lucy Gordon
The Shameless Life of Ruiz Acosta	Susan Stephens
Who Wants To Marry a Millionaire?	Nicola Marsh
Sydney Harbour Hospital: Lily's Scandal	Marion Lennox
Sydney Harbour Hospital: Zoe's Baby	Alison Roberts

HISTORICAL

The Scandalous Lord Lanchester	Anne Herries
His Compromised Countess	Deborah Hale
Destitute On His Doorstep	Helen Dickson
The Dragon and the Pearl	Jeannie Lin

MEDICAL

Gina's Little Secret	Jennifer Taylor
Taming the Lone Doc's Heart	Lucy Clark
The Runaway Nurse	Dianne Drake
The Baby Who Saved Dr Cynical	Connie Cox

Mills & Boon® Large Print

February 2012

ROMANCE

The Most Coveted Prize	Penny Jordan
The Costarella Conquest	Emma Darcy
The Night that Changed Everything	Anne McAllister
Craving the Forbidden	India Grey
Her Italian Soldier	Rebecca Winters
The Lonesome Rancher	Patricia Thayer
Nikki and the Lone Wolf	Marion Lennox
Mardie and the City Surgeon	Marion Lennox

HISTORICAL

Married to a Stranger	Louise Allen
A Dark and Brooding Gentleman	Margaret McPhee
Seducing Miss Lockwood	Helen Dickson
The Highlander's Return	Marguerite Kaye

MEDICAL

The Doctor's Reason to Stay	Dianne Drake
Career Girl in the Country	Fiona Lowe
Wedding on the Baby Ward	Lucy Clark
Special Care Baby Miracle	Lucy Clark
The Tortured Rebel	Alison Roberts
Dating Dr Delicious	Laura Iding